"I want to begin again, Sarah,"

Andres said in a gentle voice. "I want to pretend we met for the first time at the reception the other night."

"Andres I—"

"I want a chance to make up for all the harsh things I said to you that day long ago." He drew her into his arms. "I think I'm falling in love with you, Sarah."

Sarah couldn't reply. She knew there could never be anything between them. She'd made love to his brother; she'd borne his brother's child. "It's too late," she finally said. "My son and I are leaving Guadalajara in less than two weeks. We have our life, you have yours."

Sarah turned away so he wouldn't see the tears in her eyes. "It's too late for us."

But it wasn't.

Dear Reader,

Spellbinders! That's what we're striving for. The editors at Silhouette are determined to capture your imagination and win your heart with every single book we publish. Each month, six Special Editions are chosen with *you* in mind.

Our authors are our inspiration. Writers such as Nora Roberts, Tracy Sinclair, Kathleen Eagle, Carole Halston and Linda Howard—to name but a few—are masters at creating endearing characters and heart-rending love stories. Their characters are everyday people—just like you and me—whose lives have been touched by love, whose dream and desire suddenly comes true!

So find a cozy, quiet place to read, and create your own special moment with a Silhouette Special Edition.

Sincerely,

Rosalind Noonan
Senior Editor
SILHOUETTE BOOKS

BARBARA FAITH
Return to Summer

Silhouette Special Edition

Published by Silhouette Books New York

America's Publisher of Contemporary Romance

To Alfonso,
With all my love.

SILHOUETTE BOOKS
300 East 42nd St., New York, N.Y. 10017

ISBN: 0-373-09335-7

First Silhouette Books printing September 1986

America's Publisher of Contemporary Romance

Printed in the U.S.A.

Books by Barbara Faith

Silhouette Intimate Moments

The Promise of Summer #16
Wind Whispers #47
Bedouin Bride #63
Awake to Splendor #101
Islands in Turquoise #124
Tomorrow is Forever #140
Sing Me a Lovesong #146

Silhouette Special Edition

Return to Summer #335

BARBARA FAITH

is very happily married to an ex-matador whom she met when she lived in Mexico. After a honeymoon spent climbing pyramids in the Yucatán, they settled down in California—but they're vagabonds at heart. They travel at every opportunity, but Barbara always finds time to write.

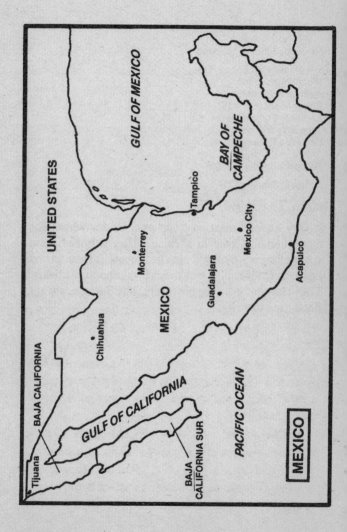

Chapter One

Sarah Maxwell had known from the minute that Richard ran into the house shouting, "Mom! I'm going to Mexico!" that she shouldn't let him go.

"Everybody in the Spanish class is going." He opened the refrigerator door. "Miss Carney and Mrs. Boseman will be chaperones. I've still got some money in the bank from when I worked last summer. It's okay, isn't it?"

He'd balanced a roll of salami, the jar of mustard, half a lemon pie and a quart of milk in his two big hands and with a grin said, "It'll be great for my Spanish because we'll be taking courses with Mexican students."

"Where ... where in Mexico?" Sarah managed to ask.

"Guadalajara. That's where you went to summer school, isn't it? Gee, it must have been great, spending two whole months in Mexico."

Sarah grabbed the pie from him and put it back in the refrigerator. "Half a sandwich," she'd said automatically. "You'll spoil your dinner."

Richard shrugged good-naturedly. "It's only for three weeks. We're all going to be staying at the hotel instead of with families. It's really going to be great, Mom. I can go, can't I?"

She'd looked at his young, eager face. He was a tall boy, already a head taller than his mother, but he hadn't quite grown into himself. Sarah knew that when he did he'd be a handsome man. Tall, dark and handsome, she thought as her stomach muscles tightened.

Richard asked so little of her that when he did request something she found it difficult to refuse. He'd worked all last summer bagging groceries, and by the beginning of the school year had made enough money to buy new school clothes and still have some left over. It wasn't that they were poor, Sarah had been with Martinez Import-Export for a long time and she made a good salary, but last summer Richard had said, "I'm not a kid anymore, Mom. I want to do my share."

She reached up and pushed a lock of hair off his forehead.

"Can I go, Mom? Please?"

It will be all right, Sarah told herself. It's only for three weeks. Richard has worked hard at school; he deserves a treat. She took a deep breath and with a smile said, "Yes, you can go. The family budget's healthy enough to pay for three weeks, so leave your money alone. Just be sure you behave your—"

With a whoop Richard picked her up and danced around the room.

So Sarah put that secret nudge of fear on the back burner of her mind. She tried to think how good it would be for Richard's Spanish and how much fun he'd have. Relax, she told herself, everything's going to be all right.

But five days before the students were supposed to leave, Rachel Carney called from the school. "Boseman has mono," Richard's teacher said. "We've got to find a replacement. You're the only mother I know who speaks Spanish, Sarah. Please—for the sake of the kids—say you'll go."

Wordlessly Sarah shook her head. Her hand tightened around the phone and she said, "I can't, Rachel. I can't."

Rachel had persisted and so had Richard. Reluctantly, hoping he'd say no, Sarah asked Pablo Hernandez if she could take her vacation now. He'd said yes, she'd earned one, and told her to bring him back a bottle of tequila and as many chili peppers as she could carry.

Now here she was, stepping out of the plane and onto the stairs, shepherding twenty-six students ahead of her, going through the long line at immigration, making sure all of the students had their tourist cards, collecting luggage and arranging for five taxis to take them into the city. Sarah was too busy to give any thought to the fact that she was actually here in Guadalajara, the city she hadn't seen for fifteen years.

She thought she'd forgotten how soft the air was, how the purple and magenta bougainvillea carpeted old stone walls, the parks and the fountains, and the rosebushes that grew five feet tall. But she hadn't forgotten, not any of it.

Even the hotel. Dear God, even the hotel was the one she'd stayed in fifteen years ago. There was no time for reflection, however, as she and Rachel herded the children into the Hotel Fénix. Sarah helped them register, frowned at Harvey Hartman when he nudged Marilee Haslip and said, "Hey, baby, how about you and me sharing a room?" and finally got everybody sorted out and into elevators.

"Is it okay if some of us go out and look around?" Richard asked.

"I guess so. But not too far from the hotel. And don't forget, I want all of you dressed and ready for the reception tonight. It starts at seven; everybody in the lobby by six forty-five."

In her own room, Sarah unpacked, then went to stand at the open windows looking down on the garden, and beyond to the street. She saw Richard, Harvey, and three other boys come out of the hotel. Smiling, she thought, I'm glad I let Richard come. I know how he feels. I remember how I felt that first day, wondering what the summer held for me.

It seemed to Sarah as she watched her son that time rolled backward, that she was seventeen again, venturing out for the first time into a strange new territory.

It had been so long ago, a lifetime ago.

"You're much too young to travel alone," her father said.

"But I won't be alone. There'll be ninety of us. We'll be chaperoned and each of us will be assigned a family to live with in Guadalajara."

"A wild and unruly people," her mother said. "Savage and undisciplined."

"That's ridiculous, Millie." Her mother's sister, Sarah's Aunt Jo, rolled her eyes heavenward. "I've been to Mexico and it's wonderful. Sarah graduates in January, then it's right off to college. I'd been looking forward to her spending the summer with me in Miami but I think this is something she'd enjoy more. You've never let her do anything, for pity's sake let her do this."

"You were going to buy me a secondhand car for my graduation," Sarah said to her father. "I'd rather have the trip to Guadalajara, Dad. Please, let me go."

The discussion had gone on for a week. Finally Sarah, with Aunt Jo's help, persuaded her mother and father to let her go. Sarah had been in a frenzy of anticipation, and when, the day before she was to leave, her aunt had slipped five twenty-dollar bills into her hand, "For something special," Sarah burst into tears.

On the plane, trying to recover from her father's orders not to take up with any of them Mex's, and her mother's warning not to drink the water, Sarah settled back into her seat and, smiling at her best friend said, "I can't believe I'm really here. It's going to be a wonderful summer, Ellie. I just know it is."

Sarah dressed carefully for the student reception that first night. She'd bought the blue dress especially for the trip and knew that it fitted her perfectly, in spite of her mother's claim that it was too tight and that she should have the next larger size. She pivoted in front of the mirror, smoothed her stockings and worried about an imaginary spot on her white pumps. Then she frowned at herself, smoothed the wisp of bangs across her wide forehead, and fluffed her shoulder-length honey-blond hair.

"Do I look all right?" she asked Ellie nervously.

"You look sensational." Tall, brown-haired Ellie Perkins grinned. "Don't worry, Sarah. You're a knockout."

"I'm so nervous. Aren't you? I wonder what our host families will be like. I hope they're nice. I hope I get a family with a couple of girls my age."

"Not me. I want one with all boys." Then Ellie hugged Sarah, and arm in arm they went downstairs where they boarded the bus that would take them to the reception.

The hall sparkled with music and color and chatter. The two girls stood for a moment at the entrance, looking about them in wonder and anticipation. The room was festooned with paper streamers and big, bright Mexican paper flowers. As a mariachi band played "Guadalajara," two hundred boys and girls tried to make themselves heard above the music.

"Señoritas?" The young woman who spoke smiled at the two girls. "I'm Alicia Moro. Register please, then I'll find your host families."

Sarah and Ellie signed and Alicia Moro said, "Ah, *sí,* Miss Maxwell and Miss Perkins. Wait here a moment please."

"I'm so excited I don't think I can stand it." Ellie squeezed Sarah's hand. "Pray for boys, Sarah. Pray I get a family of boys."

Through the crowd they saw Alicia Moro coming toward them, followed on her left by a man and a woman and four girls. On her right there were only a woman and a young man.

"My prayers have been answered," Ellie murmured. Then crossing her fingers prayed, "Please let *him* be part of my family."

But that wasn't the way it worked out.

"Señorita Perkins," Alicia Moro said, "let me present your summer family, Señor and Señora Valverde and their four daughters, Carmen, Margarita, Maria de los Angeles, and Esperanza."

For a moment Ellie was speechless. Then she gulped and managed to say, "How... how do you do?" She gave one last envious look at Sarah before the Valverde family swept her away.

"This is Señora Navarro, Sarah, and her son, Carlos," Alicia said.

"How do you do?" Sarah offered her hand.

The Señora Navarro was a tall, imposing woman, with wide dark eyes and a no-nonsense nose. Her hair was worn off her face in a chignon at her neck; her black dress was obviously expensive.

"You're rather a surprise to us, Señorita Maxwell," she told Sarah. "We expected to have a young man, but I'm afraid there was a last-minute mix-up." She frowned at Señorita Moro. "However, I'm sure things will work out and it will be a nice change for me to have a young lady in our household. I'm sorry my husband wasn't able to come tonight, but he's been ill." She hesitated, then with a look at the young man beside her said, "May I introduce my younger son, Carlos Navarro."

He was, Sarah knew, the best-looking young man she'd ever seen. Tall and slim as a reed, a few years older than she was, his face was classically handsome. He wore a dark suit and a crisp white shirt, open at the neck to show a red-and-white polka dot silk foulard cravat. His dark hair was curly and the dark eyes that appraised Sarah were filled with admiration.

"*Bienvenida* to Guadalajara." He kissed Sarah's hand and with a grin said, "So you're the little gringa who's going to spend the summer with us."

"Carlos!" Señora Navarro scowled. "That's impolite. Please remember your manners."

"Sí, mamá." The full lips twitched in smile and to Sarah he said, "Please forgive me, *señorita*. I mean no insult. May I get you a cold drink?"

Sarah, too overwhelmed to even speak, merely nodded.

The rest of the evening passed in a whirlwind of new names and faces, introductions, laughter and music. She danced with Carlos and other young men. At first she felt awkward and unsure of herself, but gradually her nervousness passed and she began to have a good time. It was fun having Carlos cut in on her time and time again, and say, "She's *my* guest this summer." Once she glimpsed Ellie dancing with an attractive boy. Ellie waved, looking far more cheerful than she had when she discovered she'd been assigned to an all girl family.

When the mariachis began to play "Strangers in the Night," Carlos leaned close to Sarah and in a low, melodic voice began to sing, *"Estranjeros en la noche,"* his lips so close that she felt the whisper of his breath against her ear. When she trembled Carlos laughed softly and said, "Relax, little gringa. I promise not to bite."

When the reception ended and it was time to say good-night, Señora Navarro said to Sarah, "My husband will come to the hotel to pick you up tomorrow morning, Miss Maxwell."

"There's no need to bother Father," Carlos put in. "I'll pick Sarah up."

Ignoring him, his mother took Sarah's hand. "Please be ready at nine," she said. Then added, "It will be pleasant having you with us this summer, Señorita Sarah."

When all of the good-nights had been said, some of the girls gathered in the windows, looking down at the street, watching their new families leave.

"How lucky can you get?" Ellie leaned her arms on the wide windowsill, gazing down at the street as Carlos helped his mother into a sleek black Cadillac. "There goes the best-looking fellow I've ever seen. You're going to have a summer to remember, Sarah."

A summer to remember. Sarah lay in bed that night gazing up at the ceiling, trying to quell the butterflies that were zipping around in her stomach. She'd only been in Mexico for two days; everything was so new, so strange. The air was fresher here, the colors more vivid, the music more lively. The men more... She thought of Carlos Navarro, of his teasing grin and his dark eyes. Of his mouth. His lips had been alarmingly close tonight, almost tickling her ear, and she'd felt...she'd felt...

She pulled the sheet up to her chin and closed her eyes, while the words of the song, "Strangers in the Night," spun round and round in her head.

The next morning at nine Sarah waited in the lobby of the Hotel Fénix, her suitcase and overnight bag on the floor beside her. At five minutes to nine the same sleek black car that she'd seen the night before pulled up in the hotel drive.

A man got out and started into the hotel. Señora Navarro had said her husband would pick Sarah up, but surely this man wasn't the señora's husband. He was twenty-six or seven Sarah thought, and though he looked like Carlos, he seemed, even at this distance, to be made of sterner stuff.

He strode into the lobby, scowling as he looked around, hands thrust into the pockets of his jeans as his black eyes skimmed over the people milling about. His gaze settled on Sarah and the jet-black brows came together in a frown.

"Miss Maxwell?"

"Yes." The word squeaked out. She cleared her throat and tried again. "I'm Sarah Maxwell. Are you...?"

"Andres Navarro, Carlos's brother," he said in English. He shook hands with her. Her hand looked small and pale and was totally enveloped in his.

"My father planned to pick you up this morning but unfortunately he was indisposed." He picked up her suitcase and overnight bag. "Are you ready?"

"Yes, thank you. I'm sorry to bother you. I hope your father will be all right."

Andres nodded, led her out to the car, opened the door on her side, then stowed her luggage in the back. He didn't speak as he pulled away from the hotel and edged the car into the heavy morning traffic.

Except that some of the buildings were older, it seemed to Sarah that downtown Guadalajara wasn't a great deal different from downtown Chicago. But the farther away from the center of town they drove the less it looked like home. The parks were summer green and when they passed one where all the trees and shrubs had been trimmed in the shape of animals— bears, giraffes, a kangaroo with a baby's head sticking out of her pouch—Sarah couldn't resist exclaiming, "Look! How cute! They're all animals."

The man beside her lifted one eyebrow. "You've never been here before?"

"No, I . . . I've never been anywhere."

"Where are you from?"

"Chicago. That's in Illinois."

"I know where it is." A battered Volkswagen darted in front of them. Andres swerved and muttered words in Spanish that Sarah had never learned in her Spanish class at Southeastern High School. Then, as though nothing had happened, he said, "I'm surprised that your parents permitted you to go so far from your home for two months."

Sarah, who'd clasped her hands together when the small car had raced by them, took a deep breath and forced herself to relax. "They didn't want me to come," she admitted. "But I—"

"You persuaded them?"

"Yes." Sarah took a deep breath. "The trip was important to me. I like Spanish. It will be my major when I start college in the fall."

"So you came to Guadalajara to study Spanish." His voice was ironic as he turned to study her face. "I've seen you American summer school girls, Miss Maxwell. I *know* how you spend your summers here, and frankly I think parents are insane to allow young women your age out of their sight without supervision."

Sarah stared at him, almost too angry to speak as he switched the radio on, presumably to drown out any retort she tried to make. She stared straight ahead, wondering why this strangely irascible man disliked her. He might be Carlos's brother but he certainly had none of his younger sibling's charm.

She looked at the hands gripping the steering wheel. They were strong hands, large but finely shaped, the nails clean and trimmed. His face in profile looked as strong as his hands. His hair was black, thick and shining clean. The eyebrows jutted out over cave-black eyes. His lips, tightened now as though in anger, were full. His jaw was firm and only saved from a look of thrusting belligerence by a rather beguiling cleft. The blue shirt was taut across his broad chest, a cashmere sweater of a deeper blue was knotted over his shoulders.

Andres Navarro, Sarah thought. He was a man, not a boy, and that frightened even as it excited her.

Fifteen minutes after they left Guadalajara he turned the car off the main highway. Here the land changed to softly rolling hills, and in the distance Sarah could see the mountains. When they came up over a rise Andres slowed the car. Below lay endless miles of green pasture land, golden fields, and cattle. To one side, almost covered by pepper and cotton-wood trees, she saw the red-tiled roof of a long white house.

"El Camichín," Andres said.

"It's beautiful." Sarah's voice was hushed. "And you've got so many cows."

One black eyebrow shot upward. "Bulls," he said. "Brave bulls raised for the bullrings of Mexico. The cows are in a different pasture beyond the hill." He glanced at Sarah. "There *is* a difference you know."

Darn the man, and darn her ignorance. Sarah looked away from him, out toward the distant moun-tains. She was a city girl; she'd never seen land like this, so vast, so endless, so forever. The golden fields were dotted with crimson poppies, wild mustard and hollyhock. Birds wheeled and darted low for seeds. A cast of hawks soared high in the blue and cloudless sky. The air smelled of summer.

Suddenly Sarah's anger faded. Inexplicably she felt the sting of tears behind her eyelids. She couldn't help it; all of her life she'd been moved by beauty. And oh, this was beautiful.

For a time neither of them spoke. Then in a quiet voice Andres said, "The *camichín* is a wild fruit that grows here in Jalisco state. It must have been a favor-ite of my great-grandfather's because that's what he named the ranch. The ranch and all of this land has been in our family for more than two hundred years. It's the most important thing in our lives."

He looked at Sarah, his face serious, almost stern. For a moment she looked back at him, her eyes as serious as his.

Señora Navarro and Carlos waited for them at the entrance of their home. "Welcome to our house," the woman said as she led Sarah into the flower-filled patio. "I'm sorry that my husband wasn't able to pick you up, but unfortunately he didn't feel well this morning. I see that Andres got you here safely."

"Yes, ma'am." Sarah looked at Carlos and smiled.

He took her hand and, as he had last night, brought it to his lips. "Let's put your bags in your room," he said. "Then I'll show you around the ranch."

"Cuca will see to Miss Maxwell's luggage," his mother said.

"No need to call her." Carlos slung Sarah's overnight bag over his shoulder, picked up her suitcase, and grabbed her hand as he led her down a long cool corridor.

The guest room was big and sunny, with French doors that opened out onto the patio. The bed, tables, chests and dressers were made of fine old wood. A thick green-and-white rug covered a large portion of the freshly scrubbed tile floor. White curtains moved in the breeze from the open windows. A bouquet of yellow roses brightened the bedside table.

"Picked 'em myself." Carlos put her suitcase on the bench at the foot of the bed. Then he glanced at her blue summer suit and shook his head. "Won't do. Haven't you got a pair of jeans?"

"Yes, of course."

"Then change. I'll wait for you on the patio." He hesitated at the door and turning back said with a grin, "Need any help?"

"No." Sarah laughed. "And close the door behind you."

Carlos was alone on the patio when she appeared twenty minutes later dressed in jeans, a shirt and sneakers.

"Hey, that's better." He grabbed her hands and whirled her around, almost spinning her off her feet. Sarah tried to regain her balance as she grabbed his shoulders, laughing up at him as his hands tightened on her waist.

Then over his shoulder she saw Andres. He stood, hands on narrow hips, watching them. His eyes were hard, his lips narrowed into a tight line of anger.

Sarah's breath caught in her throat as she broke away from Carlos. She suddenly felt a chill of apprehension. Why had he looked at her that way?

Chapter Two

"We shall speak only Spanish from now on, Sarah," Señora Navarro said that night at dinner. "If there is something you don't understand please feel free to interrupt and say, *'Momento, habla más despacio,'* and we'll speak more slowly."

"Muy bien, señora." She couldn't imagine herself ever interrupting Andres Navarro, Sarah thought as she glanced at him across the table. Averting her eyes she took a sip of her wine. Apparently it was the custom here to serve wine with dinner. She'd have to be careful because she wasn't used to it. She wasn't accustomed to so many things.

"Let's not begin by making things too difficult for Sarah," Federico Navarro said. He reached over to pat

Sarah's hand. "You are our adopted daughter for this summer, my dear. We want you to feel at home."

"Thank you, Señor Navarro." Sarah had liked him the moment she'd met him in the *sala* this evening before dinner. He was a frail man, smaller in stature than either of his sons. His hair was snowy white, his hands were speckled with age, but his eyes, though faded with illness, were warm and lively.

He was the only one in the family that Sarah truly felt comfortable with. Teresa Navarro had told her the first night that they had expected a young man, so obviously she disapproved of Sarah's presence.

Almost as much as Andres did. Sarah looked up to see him watching her again. Why did he dislike her? she wondered. Why was he so angry that she was here?

Carlos, of course, more than made up for Andres's animosity. He was overly friendly, and she was far too inexperienced to know what to do about it.

With a sigh Sarah thought of all the statistics she'd read about teenage girls and the fact that such a high percentage of them lost their virginity by the time they were sixteen. She wasn't one of them. She hadn't even been allowed to date until she was sixteen and even then all of her dates had been supervised. "Who is he?" her father had asked every time Sarah had a date. "Where does he live? No, you may not go out on a weeknight, and you may not set one foot in his car. You'll take the bus or I'll drive you." He'd made her dates uncomfortable with his questions and only one or two had had the temerity to ask her out a second time.

Now here she was in a foreign country, sitting next to one of the best-looking young men she'd ever seen, and it scared her. *He* scared her.

Sarah took another sip of her wine and tried to follow the conversation. She'd done well in a classroom atmosphere, but this was different. She felt lost, adrift in a sea of conversation, catching only a few words. Even the food was strange. She'd never had tortilla soup before—she'd never had a tortilla before.

"We're having Chicken Pipián," Teresa Navarro said. "I hope you like it."

"I'm sure I will." Sarah smiled, relieved that she'd be eating something she was familiar with.

A maid entered, carrying a platter covered with a thick green sauce and Señora Navarro said, "Please serve Señorita Maxwell a breast."

Sarah looked down at her plate as the maid served her. She couldn't even see the chicken, all she could see was the thick green, oozing sauce. She looked up and saw Andres watching her with a mocking, challenging smile. She picked up her fork and taking a deep breath cut through the sauce into the chicken. It was delicious, tangy and sharp, totally unlike anything Sarah had ever tasted. She took another bite and smiled sweetly at Andres.

"Let me fix you a tortilla." Señor Navarro took one from the covered basket, filled it with white country

cheese, a bit of Mexican *salsa* and a sprinkle of pars-
leylike greenery. He rolled it up and handed it to her.

"Gracias," Sarah said as she bit into it, then
gasped.

"I put too much *salsa* in," Señor Navarro said.
"I'm sorry, I'll fix you another."

"No." Sarah reached for her glass of water. "It's
wonderful." And it was. Everything was, strange and
different, but the best food she'd ever tasted. She finished the chicken breast and had two more tortillas.
That night she slept better than she had in a long time.

The next week was spent getting acquainted with the
new school and students. Every morning at eight she
and Carlos drove the fifteen miles into Guadalajara in
his red Volkswagen bug. He was a fast driver, but so
it seemed was everyone else in Mexico. He handled the
small car well, and with the canvas top down and the
sun shining on her face, Sarah relaxed. Carlos was at-
tentive and he was fun to be with. It was going to be a
wonderful summer.

She liked her classes and within a week spoke
Spanish fluently and without even thinking about it.
If she made a mistake in grammar she plunged on,
knowing that the most important thing was to com-
municate.

"This is great, isn't it?" Ellie said one morning as
they slid into their seats. "I love Guadalajara and my
new family. Remember how I complained about having to live with four girls? Well, *amiga*, the girls all
have boyfriends that have boyfriends. I've met a lot of

really cute guys and I know it's going to be some kind of a summer." She lowered her voice to a whisper. "Speaking of cute guys, Carlos Navarro is the best-looking one I've ever seen. You'd better watch yourself with him, Sarah. I think he's been around a lot more than you have." She grinned at Sarah. "My God, wouldn't your dad drop his teeth if he knew you were living with him?"

"I'm not living with him. I'm living with his family, and that includes an older brother who's mean as a snake and watches every move I make. Believe me, Ellie, even if I wanted to I couldn't get into any trouble. I'm almost never alone with Carlos."

"Never?"

"Well . . . We drive back and forth to school every day of course."

"Of course." Ellie grinned at her.

Sarah longed to say something to Ellie about the way Carlos behaved, but although Ellie was her best friend, she felt awkward about discussing anything so personal. She'd have felt like a sappy kid saying, "He's too much for me. I don't know how to handle him. What should I do?"

It had started the first week Sarah was at El Cami-chín. She enjoyed the mild flirting, when she knew his family was close by, but she was nervous about being alone with Carlos. He knew it and teased her about it.

"Don't be afraid of me, Sarita," he said. "I'd never do anything you didn't want me to do. But there isn't any harm in a few kisses, is there? Think of it as cementing Mexican-American relations.''

The first time Carlos pulled off the road to El Camichín and parked close to the trees, Sarah said, ''What are you doing?''

''I'm tired.'' He turned the dial of the radio until he found a station with a slower rock beat. ''I thought it'd be nice to sit here for a few minutes and relax. Just the two of us. I never see you alone at school and when we're at home my mother watches me like a hawk.''

''So does your brother.''

A look of fleeting discomfort crossed his handsome face. ''That's because I'm seven years younger than he is. He still thinks I'm a kid.'' He moved closer to Sarah. ''But I'm not, *muchacha*, I'm almost twenty-one. And I think you're just about the cutest little thing I've ever seen.''

''Carlos...''

''Now be still and kiss me.'' He kissed her, then laughed as Sarah scooted as far over on her side of the small car as she could get. He reached out to curl a strand of blond hair around one finger, then tugged her to him.

''We'd better go,'' she said nervously.

''In a minute.'' Carlos urged her closer, one hand around the back of her neck, and kissed her again.

It was nice. It was *very* nice. When he let her go Sarah looked at him, her lips parted, her heart beating in time to the slow rock.

''Once more,'' he said.

"No, we'd better—"

But his lips, so warm and young, met hers again. "Sarah," he murmured, and reached for her breasts.

"No!" She pulled out of his arms. "You stop that, Carlos. You just stop that right now."

His eyes were hot, his nostrils flared, and she was afraid for a moment that he was angry. Instead he laughed. "Okay," he said. "For this time."

Sarah liked kissing him. It was fun sitting in the little red car—so far from her parents' disapproving influence—with a young man as exciting as Carlos Navarro. She liked hearing the low gasp of his breath against her lips, knowing that she excited him. It frightened her but there was a feeling of exhilaration in the fear that made her feel more alive than she'd ever felt before.

It became a game with Carlos, a game that he was determined to win. Sarah knew she was on dangerous ground, that sometime she might not be able to stop him. But she liked Carlos, and although she admitted to herself that she was a little afraid of him, she found the challenge of fending him off as exciting as his kisses.

But every time he tried to touch her, Sarah pulled away.

"Come on," he always said. "What can it hurt? Don't be that way, Sarah. You're so sweet, so soft."

Once again Sarah would relax, but when he tried to touch her she'd break away. Each time they parked they stayed longer and longer. The kisses grew more ardent. There were times when Sarah held him away that he grew angry. Then he'd push her over to her own side of the car and wheel out of the grove of trees, too upset to speak. I've ruined it, she'd think. He's through with me, he'll never kiss me again.

The next day Carlos would pull off the road as though nothing had happened, and urge Sarah into his arms. She managed to hold him away when he tried to touch her—until the night of the Fourth of July party.

"In honor of our American students," the head of the school said, "we're having an all-day picnic at Lake Chapala."

Buses were provided for students who didn't have cars, and that's the way that Ellie, accompanied by her four "summer sisters," went to the picnic. But Sarah went with Carlos in the red Volkswagen.

The day was bright and sunny. The lake—thirty-two miles from Guadalajara—was warm. The students swam and boated. They also ate great quantities of fried chicken, tamales, tacos, and potato salad. Late in the afternoon Carlos insisted he teach Sarah how to water-ski. It took half a dozen attempts before she finally wobbled out on the water. She managed to stay up for a minute or two before she fell. Carlos, skiing next to her, fell deliberately so he could help her. They came back to shore and he insisted she try again. This time she stayed up and it was wonderful.

When she finally came in to give someone else a chance on the skis, she took a cola and sat on the sand next to Ellie.

"You'd better keep an eye on Carlos," Ellie said.

"Why?" Sarah's eyebrows rose in question.

"He's had about a zillion beers, that's why."

"Not a zillion." Sarah's voice was defensive. "Anyway, all of the fellows are drinking."

"But not all of them have to drive." Ellie looked worried. "Maybe you'd better come back on the bus with us."

Sarah shook her head. "No, I wouldn't do that. Carlos will be all right, Ellie."

But by the time they were ready to start for home Carlos's face was flushed, and when he opened the car door he staggered.

"Maybe we'd better go on the bus," Sarah said. "We could come back for the car tomorrow."

"Don't be silly. I'm per...perfectly all right."

She looked at the other students, boarding the bus now. "Will you let me drive?" she said.

"The bug?" Carlos laughed. "Have you ever driven a stick shift?"

"No, but..."

He laughed, then pulling her into his arms, kissed her. "Don't worry, Sarita, I'll get us home safely."

The traffic on the highway going back to Guadalajara was heavy. Carlos drove too fast. "Keeping up with everybody else," he said when Sarah pleaded with him to slow down.

More afraid than she'd ever been in her life, all that Sarah could do was tighten her seat belt and pray. She vowed that never again would she get into a car with someone who'd been drinking. When they finally turned off the highway onto the road leading to El Camichín she breathed a sigh of relief. She'd just unclasped her fear-damp hands when Carlos reached for her.

"Why are you sitting so far away?" he asked.

"Carlos, please, be careful."

"S'all right, sweetheart. Old Carlos knows what he's doing." He put his hand on her thigh. "Glad you wore a skirt today, Sarah. You've got great legs and the smoothest skin of any girl I've ever known. You've got everything, Sarah, and I want it. 'Bout time I had it too."

Without warning he jerked the car to the side of the road and stopped. "C'mere," he said.

Sarah didn't like this. Carlos was drunk. She wanted to get safely back to her room, away from him, away from the hands that reached for her.

"Want you," he mumbled as he pulled her to him for a frantic open-mouth kiss.

"No!" Sarah tried to squirm away but he only laughed and reached for her again. One hand grasped the back of her neck to urge her forward, the other hand found her breasts.

"Soft," he gasped against her mouth. "Stop struggling, my little *gringita*, you know you like this as much as I do."

The hand on her breasts made her feel strange and tingly. Sarah wanted him to stop but at the same time she felt a surge of excitement and for a moment she relaxed against him. His other hand moved down to her leg and suddenly, before Sarah knew what was happening, up under her skirt. With an outraged gasp she tugged his hand away.

"You stop that!" she cried.

"Got to touch you." He tried to break free of her grasp, but Sarah held onto his wrist, struggling with him until he said, "Damn little tease. Leading me on, making me think you want me as much as I want you and then you stop." Carlos pulled away from her and slid back under the wheel. "Ice princess from the frozen north," he muttered angrily as he started the car, and with a wrench yanked it back on the road.

Suddenly, out of the shadowy trees, a horse darted out in front of the car. Sarah screamed as Carlos jerked the wheel. The car lurched sickeningly, then skidded across the road. It missed the horse by inches, sideswiped a tree, and slid sideways into a ditch.

"Dios!" Carlos shook his head as though to clear it. "Damned horse. You okay?"

"I . . . I think so." Sarah's voice shook. She looked at Carlos and saw a trickle of blood on his forehead. "You're hurt," she gasped. "Are you all right?"

"Yeah, sure." He groaned. "I'm . . ." He slumped over the wheel.

"Carlos?" Sarah touched his shoulder. He didn't answer her. For a moment she looked at him, then quickly got out of the car. She had to get help, she had to . . .

"¿Qué pasa?" she heard somebody call and saw a man running toward her. "Are you all right? Is that the young Señor Navarro's car?"

"Yes. He's hurt. Please, can you get help?"

"Sí, sí. I'll tell them at the *casa."* Without waiting for a reply the man disappeared into the darkness.

Sarah got back into the car. Carlos was still slumped over the wheel. She spoke to him but he didn't answer. She got out of the car again.

The stillness of the night was broken only by the sound of crickets. What if Carlos was badly hurt? she thought frantically. What if he . . . ? He has to be all right, she told herself. He has to be.

She paced up and down the road and finally she saw the lights of a car. When it stopped Andres jumped out and ran to her.

"What in the hell happened?" he snapped.

"A horse," she managed to say. "He ran in front of us. Carlos is—"

But Andres had shoved her aside as he opened the car door. Quickly and carefully he eased Carlos out and laid him on the ground beside the car. He knelt down and ran his hands over his brother's body. In the reflection of the headlights he saw the wound. He put a clean white handkerchief against it. "Carlos?" he said. "Carlos, can you hear me?"

"'Course I can hear you, big brother." Carlos tried to sit up, but with a groan he slumped back. "Holy saints," he mumbled. "Head hurts."

Andres stared down at his brother. "It should hurt!" He stood up and glared at Sarah. "He smells like a damn brewery. How much did he drink?"

"I . . . I don't know. Six or seven beers maybe."

"And you?" He was furious now. "How many did you have?"

"None. I . . . I don't drink."

"I bet you don't." He grabbed her shoulders and brought his face close to hers.

Sarah looked up at him as his hands tightened on her arms. His face was only inches from hers, his cave-dark eyes were narrowed in anger. She could feel his breath on her cheeks. His lips were slightly parted, his body tense.

"Please," Sarah whispered. "Please, I—"

Andres's lips brushed hers. She trembled under the hands that held her and he let her go. "Just . . . testing for alcohol," he said in a low voice. "I'm sorry. I didn't ask if you were all right. Are you?"

No, Sarah wanted to say. I'm not all right. I don't think I'll ever breathe properly again. You shouldn't have held me like that. You shouldn't have kissed me.

"I'm all right." Sarah straightened her shoulders and stepped away from him.

Andres nodded, then turned back to Carlos. He bent down, lifted his younger brother to his feet, and slung him over his shoulder. "Come along," he said to Sarah, "we'd better get the two of you back to the house."

There was no school the next day, which was a good thing because Carlos wasn't in any condition to go. He had a nasty bump on his head and his mother, over his protests, insisted he be seen by a doctor. His father had given him a good talking-to about drinking and driving and most of all about endangering their guest.

"You could have killed both yourself and Sarah," Federico said. "I hope you've apologized to her."

"I have, *papá*." Carlos winked at Sarah.

The morning after the accident Carlos had knocked on the French doors of her bedroom. When Sarah opened the doors Carlos smiled his irresistible smile and said, "I'm sorry, Sarah. Maybe I'd better teach you how to drive the bug. You sure you're all right?"

"Yes, Carlos. I'm fine."

"It was all your fault, you know."

"My fault?" Sarah's eyes widened.

"You're a tantalizing little witch, gringa. I can't keep my hands off you. If you'd given in to me last night we wouldn't have had the accident. You're a tease, Sarah, and you're driving me crazy." Before she could back into the room he grabbed her and his body, so straight and slim and young, moved against hers.

Suddenly Sarah knew she didn't want to play this game any longer. She didn't want Carlos to touch her, not even to kiss her.

Kiss her he did nonetheless, and when he let her go he said, "I'm warning you, Sarita, before summer's over I'm going to have you. I know you want me just

as much as I want you so don't keep playing the innocent too long or I'll lose my patience.''

He put his finger under her chin and raised her face
to his. ''You weren't raised in a convent, Sarah.
You've been around, you know what the score is.'' His
fingers tightened on her chin, hurting her. ''We both
know how we feel, Sarah. It's time we did something
about our feelings.''

Sarah knew that she was out of her depth. A situa-
tion had to be handled and she hadn't the slightest
notion in the world how to tackle it.

Chapter Three

The patio of the Navarro home glowed in the light of dozens of lanterns and candelabra. The sound of cicadas and night birds filled the air.

Soon the guests would arrive, mariachis would begin to play, and the sound of laughter and of congratulations would be heard. For tonight was a happy occasion; the younger Navarro son was twenty-one.

Two weeks had passed since the accident. Carlos hadn't been at all chagrined by what had happened. If anything he seemed more determined than ever in his efforts to seduce Sarah; but she was more cautious now, less willing to play the game.

Tonight, however, was his birthday and Sarah wanted to look nice. With the money Aunt Jo had given her, she and Ellie, who'd been invited to the Navarro party along with the four young ladies in her host family, went shopping in Guadalajara. Sarah had tried on at least a dozen dresses before she settled on a simple white cotton lace frock. The neckline was lower than she was accustomed to, but when she hesitated Ellie said, "The dress is perfect, Sarah, your mother would hate it."

Sarah grinned and said, "I'll take it."

With it Sarah wore high-heeled white sandals and a blue shell necklace and earrings. Just before she left her room that night one of the Navarro maids knocked on her door and handed her one perfect fresh gardenia.

Sarah smiled as she accepted it. Then she stood in front of the mirror, rebrushed her blond hair, and as she fastened the gardenia behind one ear, thought how nice it was of Carlos to think of the flower.

When she went outside the patio was already filled with people of all ages—older family relatives, contemporaries of Señor and Señora Navarro, and classmates whom Sarah recognized from school. For a moment, overcome by shyness, she lingered in the doorway.

At home she'd been allowed to go to only a few school dances, so Sarah had never gained the self-confidence of most young women her age. Now she stood, partly hidden by the shadows, tapping her foot to the music, until a voice said, "Would you care to dance?" It was Andres, dressed in black trousers, a black silk shirt, and a white dinner jacket that made his wide shoulders look even broader.

With the mocking smile she knew so well he offered her his arm. Sarah put her hand tentatively on his sleeve as she followed him to where the others were dancing. He put his arms around her. "You look nice, Miss Sarah," he said.

"Thank you." She looked up at him, then focused her eyes on his shoulder.

"You're trembling." He sounded surprised. "Do I frighten you?"

"No. I . . . I'm not used to dancing," she said truthfully.

"No? I'd have thought that a girl as attractive as you would be accomplished at dancing as well as a lot of other things." When Sarah didn't answer his arms tightened around her.

They didn't speak then, and after a few moments Sarah began to relax enough to give herself up to the music and to the arms that held her. She didn't think that Andres liked her; she didn't think she liked him. Yet she felt a strange comfort in being in his arms.

He let her go when the music stopped. With the same mocking smile he touched her hair, brushing his fingers against the gardenia as he said, almost to himself, "You really are quite lovely, Miss Sarah Maxwell."

Then he led her back to where he'd found her and another young man, a friend of Carlos's from school, claimed her. But they had no more than stepped out to dance when Carlos cut in. "It's *my* birthday," he told his friend. "Tonight Sarah belongs to me." As he danced her away he said, "Are you going to kiss me happy birthday?"

"Of course." She smiled and stood on tiptoe to kiss his cheek. "There you are. Happy birthday, Carlos. Thank you for the gardenia."

"The gardenia?" He looked surprised. "I didn't send it."

"Oh?" Sarah stared at him. "Then perhaps your father did." But she knew, deep down she knew who had sent it. Although she didn't know why.

"You can give me a proper kiss later," Carlos said, breaking in on her thoughts. "That'll be my birthday present, ice princess. I deserve more than a peck on the cheek, Sarah, and believe me, I mean to collect later." Playfully he nipped her ear and said, "Come on, let's have a glass of wine."

He took her hand, but as they neared the refreshment table he hesitated. Then with a shrug he muttered, "Damn." His hand tightened on hers when they reached the table where Andres and a fragile young woman, very close to Sarah's age, waited.

"Good evening, Maria," Carlos said politely. "How nice you look tonight. May I introduce our summer student? Miss Sarah Maxwell. Sarah, this is Maria Escobar."

Maria Escobar smiled shyly as she took Sarah's hand. Dressed in a pale pink gown, with a neckline far more discreet than Sarah's, her raven-black hair was worn straight back off her small face and held in place by a high Spanish comb. She looked every inch a Latin lady.

Maria seemed too young for Andres. But perhaps, Sarah thought, he liked his women young so that he could intimidate them the way he intimidated her. She glanced at Carlos. He flushed and looked away.

"Maria has only just arrived, Carlos," Andres said. "She hasn't had an opportunity to dance yet."

Carlos's eyes flared in momentary anger before he said, "Then of course we must remedy that." He offered Maria his hand and with a forced smile said, "Shall we?"

"What a pretty girl," Sarah said. "Does she live near here?"

"Her family owns the ranch adjoining El Camichín. She and Carlos have known each other since they were children." He handed Sarah a glass of white wine. "When do you return to Chicago?"

"At the end of August."

"That's almost a month from now."

"Yes." Sarah took a sip of her wine.

"Carlos is just a boy, you know. He needs a firm hand to keep him in line."

"Then isn't he lucky to have you for his older brother." Sarah smiled, but her hand shook when she raised her glass. What was Andres trying to tell her? To leave Carlos alone? Darn it, why didn't he tell his brother to leave *her* alone? Without thinking Sarah drained her glass.

"Would you care for another?"

"Please."

"I thought you didn't drink."

"I don't. I mean...well wine isn't really drinking, is it?"

"Isn't it?" He handed her a glass.

She took a sip as she turned away to watch the dancing couples. She saw Ellie, eyes closed, dancing with a young man Sarah had never met. Her gaze moved to Maria Escobar and Carlos. She took another sip of wine, feeling a momentary twinge of jealousy. When she raised her glass again Andres took it out of her hand.

"You've had enough," he said. "Let's dance." Before Sarah could object he led her out to the center of the patio.

The lights were dimmer now, the music softer. The scent of jasmine and orange blossoms filled the air. When Andres put his arms around her, Sarah, without being aware of what she was doing, rested her head against his shoulder, wondering as she did why it felt so good to be held by this strange and taciturn man. He'd let her know from almost the beginning that he didn't like her. Yet his hand felt warm against her back, and the arms that held her gave her a feeling of security she'd never felt before.

Sarah closed her eyes. The smooth fabric of the white jacket felt good against her cheek. She turned her face slightly into the warmth of his neck, breathing in his clean male smell. His fingers moved against her back, soothing, caressing. She felt the brush of his chin against her hair as his hand tightened on hers. With a sigh she moved closer.

"Sarah?"

She opened her eyes and slowly looked up at him, caught by the intensity of his gaze. "Sarah, I . . ."

Carlos tapped his shoulder. "My turn, big brother," he said. Before Sarah could speak, Carlos swept her away.

"It's my birthday," he said. "You're my girl. I don't want you dancing with anybody but me from now on."

Sarah didn't see Andres for the rest of the evening. She danced every dance with Carlos and when the musicians left she let him lead her over to the few tables still occupied by their friends from school. Ellie was with the young man who had been her dancing partner earlier. They all drank another glass of wine, and finally, at a little after two, the party ended.

When Carlos walked Sarah down the corridor to her room he said, "I'll collect that birthday kiss now."

She submitted to his kiss and when he stepped away he looked at her and said, "What's the matter?"

"Nothing, Carlos. I'm tired, that's all. It's been quite an evening; I think I had too much wine." Before he could speak she went in and closed the door.

For a few moments Sarah stood there in the darkness. A soft breeze stirred the curtains; the scent of jasmine drifted into the room. She took the gardenia out of her hair and held it to her face before she laid it on the bedside table. Then she undressed, got into bed and snapped off the light.

Sarah lay for a long time, listening to the quiet night sounds, and just before she closed her eyes reached out and touched the delicate petals of the gardenia.

She was almost asleep when she heard a sharp scrape, then a click. Her eyes flew open just as a figure stepped through the French doors.

"Who is it? What do you want?" She pulled the sheet up to her neck to cover herself. "Who is it?" she said again. "I'll scream. I'll—"

"Shh! It's me, Carlos. Do you want to wake up the whole house?"

"What do you want?"

"What do you think I want?" Before Sarah could stop him he lay down beside her and pulled her into his arms.

"No, don't—"

Carlos stopped her words with a kiss. "Sarita," he breathed against her lips. "My sweet little gringa."

Sarah felt as though her heart would jump out of her body. She tried to move away from him but he held her, his hand against her hair as his mouth covered hers. "You've been driving me crazy for days," he said against her lips. "I can't stand it, Sarah." His voice was blurred by wine and desire, his mouth was insistent. "I'm through waiting, Sarah, I have to have you, honey. I have to."

"Carlos, please stop it." She put her hands against his chest, trying to hold him away.

"Just kiss me, Sarah. Just for a minute. Please, honey."

She clutched the sheet tighter against her body. Then the sheet wasn't there, Carlos had pulled it away, just as he was now pulling her nightgown aside.

"No! What are you—?"

He silenced her with a kiss and pressed his body to hers. Sarah struggled away from him. "Carlos, please. You've got to stop."

"I can't stop, Sarah, not now." He pulled the gown up over her hips. She could feel the hardness of him against her leg. She didn't want this.

"It's all right, sweetheart. I love you, Sarah. You know I love you."

"Carlos, please." With every bit of her strength Sarah tried to push him away.

"Dammit, Sarah! I've listened to your 'don'ts' and your 'not nows' and your 'stop its' long enough. Maybe you can treat your Chicago boyfriends this way, but you can't do this to me." He straddled her, his legs holding her tight while he tossed his robe aside. "I don't want to hurt you. Just stop pretending you don't want this as much as I do. You've teased me long enough, now it's time to pay up."

It was awful. It hurt a lot. That's all Sarah felt—the pain, the weight of his body, her own terrible embarrassment.

When it was over Carlos rolled away from her. For a long time he didn't speak. At last he said, "I'm sorry. I didn't think you were a virgin."

When Sarah didn't answer he got up, put on his robe, and left her alone.

She lay for a long time, motionless, her eyes squeezed shut, trying to blot everything out of her mind. When finally she sat up she saw the gardenia on the floor, crushed and broken by Carlos's foot.

Sarah bent to pick it up and it was then that she began to weep.

Chapter Four

For the next few days Sarah avoided Carlos. She told Señora Navarro that she didn't feel well and that she'd like to stay home from school. Confused and bewildered, not wanting to see anyone, she didn't even come out of her room for meals.

On the fourth morning after the birthday party Andres knocked on her bedroom door.

"Feeling better?" he asked when Sarah opened the door.

"Yes, thank you." She wouldn't look directly at him.

"I thought it was time you had some fresh air. How'd you like to go horseback riding? You do ride, don't you?"

"Yes, but—"

"Good. Change your clothes and meet me at the stable." Before she could reply Andres turned and hurried back down the corridor.

Sarah didn't want to go riding with him. She wanted to stay right here in her room, hidden away from people, forever. For years she'd dreamed about how wonderful it would be to give yourself to the man you loved. She hadn't been sure just how it would feel, but she knew it must be beautiful.

Giving, yes; but being *taken*? It hadn't been beautiful at all. It had been painful and ugly. After it was over she'd felt soiled and ashamed. She never wanted to see Carlos Navarro again.

She wished she'd had the courage to tell Andres that she didn't want to go riding with him, she didn't want to go anywhere with him. But he was so big and somehow fierce looking, that she was afraid if she refused he'd pick her up, sling her over his shoulder, and carry her down to the stable.

Mumbling to herself, Sarah yanked on a pair of jeans and pulled a T-shirt over her head. Darn him anyway, she thought. Darn all the darn Navarros.

Andres was waiting for her when Sarah got to the stable. He saw her rebellious face but he didn't. say anything as he led her over to the gentle brown mare he'd saddled for her. He helped her mount, then adjusted her stirrups and said, "Comfortable?"

Sarah nodded and tightened her hands on the reins.

They didn't speak as they started off. For a while they rode side by side, but as they began to climb they went single file, with Andres leading the way. It felt good to be outside in the fresh clean air, and for the first time since Sarah had known Andres, she felt almost comfortable with him. He sat straight in the saddle, one hand loosely holding the reins of the big gray gelding, a thoughtful, determined look on his face.

As they climbed higher the air turned cool, but when Andres asked her if she needed a sweater, Sarah shook her head. She loved the coolness, the scent of the pines, the feel of the horse under her. For the first time since *it* had happened she felt the tension ease. She didn't know where Andres was taking her but it didn't matter. Out here she felt free.

As he led her through scraggly trees and underbrush he said, "Be careful, watch your head. We've only got a short way to go now." When they reached a clearing he stopped and dismounted, then reached up to help Sarah off her horse.

"Let's go over this way," he said. "I want to show you something."

Sarah followed him through the clearing to an outcrop of rocks. Andres didn't speak to her for a long moment, he just stood there, feet apart, his eyes narrowed against the morning sun.

"There it is," he said at last as he pointed below. "El Camichín."

Sarah looked to where he had pointed, to the golden fields and the rolling green pastureland. In the distance, barely visible through the trees, she could see the red tile roof of the house.

"It's beautiful, Andres," Sarah said. "It must have been wonderful growing up here."

He nodded. "This land has belonged to the Navarro family for over two hundred years. I told you that, didn't I, the day I brought you to El Camichín?" He gestured off to the left. "That's Escobar land."

Maria Escobar, Sarah thought, the girl I met the night of the birthday party.

"Land is important to us," Andres went on, "as important as carrying on the family name." He looked at Sarah. "I was injured by a bull when I was fourteen. I can never father children. It will be up to Carlos to carry on the name of Navarro through his sons." He waited, watching Sarah.

Why was he telling her this? She felt the cold suddenly and hugged her arms close to her body.

"I've watched you and Carlos," Andres said. "I haven't liked what I've seen. I know this flirtation between the two of you isn't entirely your fault, Sarah. Carlos is young and he's headstrong. God knows he can be charming when he wants to be. I know too that things are different in your country than they are here. You set a different value on...on some things." He looked uncomfortable. "I'm well aware that many young American women find nothing wrong in having a few... experiences before they marry."

"That's not true." Sarah's face had gone white. "You don't know. You can't judge—"

"I'm not judging. I'm just pointing out the differences in our two cultures. A Mexican girl would never be allowed the kind of freedom American girls have." He moved a step closer to her. "Carlos likes you, Sarah. But believe me, it's only a summer romance. It will be over the moment you step on that plane for the States. Can't you see that, Sarah? You're here and you're easy and—"

"Stop it!" Sarah covered her face with her hands. "Oh, please, stop it."

Andres took her hands and pulled them away from her face. "He's betrothed to Maria Escobar," he said in a stern voice. "I'm sorry he hasn't seen fit to tell you. He should have. They'll be married next year and when they do a part of the Escobar land will come to the marriage. It's important to both families that our land, as well as our blood—Mexican blood—be joined." His hands tightened on Sarah's wrists. "Nothing, Sarah, absolutely nothing is going to interfere with the marriage. Do you understand?"

Sarah stared up at Andres, too shocked, too hurt to reply, conscious only of the chill in the air and the whisper of the wind through the pines. Then, feeling as though she'd been physically bruised, she broke free from Andres and stumbled blindly away.

He caught her just as she reached the trees. "Sarah, I'm sorry. I didn't mean to hurt you, but you had to know."

"Let me go," she pleaded as she turned her face away. Let me go away from myself, away from my shame and my foolishness, she begged wordlessly.

Slowly Andres turned her around to face him. "I know you care about Carlos," he said, "but believe me, Sarah, you'll forget about him when you're back home among your own friends." He touched the side of her face. "Don't look like that," he said in a low voice. Without even knowing that he was going to, he put his arms around her. "You'll go home in a few weeks," he murmured against her hair. "You'll forget Carlos."

Sarah wanted to hold onto him. She wanted to weep against his shoulder and tell him that Carlos had taken away her girlhood and that she was sorry, that she wished with all her heart it had never happened.

"Sarah," Andres said again, and kissed her.

Her lips quivered against his. She thought he said her name again, then she didn't think at all.

She hadn't known a kiss could be like this, that it could rock her right down to her toes and make the blood sing through her veins. It was a kiss that was fierce and possessive, yet strangely gentle. It awoke feelings that Sarah had not even imagined.

Her arms crept up around Andres's neck. When his tongue edged against her lips her breath caught in her throat. She molded her body closer to his and felt the long male length of him against her. For the first time in her life she knew what desire was.

Then it was over. He held her away from him. His eyes were dark and hooded, his nostrils fluted with passion. She felt the pressure of his strong fingers digging into her upper arms.

He let her go and stepped away from her. "We'd better head back," he said in an emotion-harsh voice. "It's time. It's past time."

Sarah left Guadalajara the next day. She told Señora Navarro that she was homesick, and asked Señor Navarro to drive her to the airport. Carlos was in school when she left; Andres had gone to Jocotepec to look at some new stock.

Her parents were glad to see her but they couldn't understand why Sarah had returned home before the summer term ended. She couldn't tell them. She couldn't say, "I've been a fool. You were right, I should never have left home."

She tried not to think about what had happened between her and Carlos, and found that after a while she could put the memory of it out of her mind— but not the memory of Andres's kiss.

In the first week of September Sarah began the last half of her senior year. By October she knew that she was pregnant, and the only person she confided in was Ellie.

Ellie burst into tears when Sarah told her. "What are you going to do?" she wailed. "Oh, Sarah, what are you going to do?"

"I don't know." She was too frightened, too sick at heart to think straight.

"You've got to tell your parents."

"I can't. They'll never forgive me."

"Of course they will. I know they're strict, Sarah, but they're your parents. They love you."

So Sarah told them and it was awful. In despair, urgently needing someone to talk to, Sarah called her Aunt Jo in Miami. And that's where she had gone, the day after she received her high school diploma.

Richard had been born the end of April. It was a difficult delivery, but Sarah knew from the moment that her son was placed in her arms that whatever she'd gone through had been worth it. Richard was hers and she loved him.

As soon as she was on her feet she told her aunt she was going to get a job and that as soon as she could she'd find an apartment for herself and Richard.

"You'll do no such thing," Jo Kelsey said. "You're going to college."

"But I can't now. I've got a baby to take care of."

"Then you can take care of him before and after school. I'll take care of him the rest of the time." Jo gripped Sarah's hands. "This is important," she said. "Go to college and get your degree so that you'll be equipped for the job market. I don't want you waiting on tables for the rest of your life."

So Sarah had gone to the University of Miami and she and Richard had lived with her aunt until she graduated. Then, with a major in business and a minor in Spanish, she'd gotten a job with a Latin American import-export company. She'd been with them for the last fourteen years and had risen to be their first woman vice-president.

Now here she was, fifteen years later, in Guadalajara, the city she'd vowed never to return to.

Sarah wore her hair shorter now, but it was almost the same honey-blond shade it had been fifteen years before. That night, as she fastened on amber earrings almost the same shade as her eyes she looked at herself in the mirror and thought, I'll only be here for three weeks. Nothing will happen.

She smoothed the lime-green dress down over her hips, wondering, as she always did, if the neckline was too revealing. She tried not to think about the reception because it reminded her of that first reception so long ago.

Thirty minutes later she stood at the threshold of the big salon, feeling a wave of nostalgia. It's just the same she thought; nothing has changed. There were the same paper streamers, the same brightly colored paper flowers. Even the mariachis were playing all of the old songs Sarah had grown to love.

"I can't believe I'm really here," Richard said. "Was it the same, Mom, when you were here I mean?"

"Yes, it was the same."

"It's great, isn't it."

"Hey, c'mon." Harvey grabbed Richard's arm. "Let's find ourselves a couple of girls."

"Grow up, man." Richard grinned at Sarah. "Will you excuse me, Mom? I'd better keep an eye on this guy. He's a real animal."

"Sure," she said. "You go ahead. I want to check with Rachel."

But Sarah didn't move from where she stood, content for the moment to watch the milling crowd of students. They weren't much different than they'd been fifteen years ago, she thought. The boys had worn their hair longer then. Today, except for a few of the Mexican girls, both boys and girls wore their hair short. But otherwise they were the same. Everything was the same.

She turned away finally, thinking to look for Rachel as she tried to make her way through the crowd of parents and chaperones.

"Excuse me," a man said as he shouldered past her. "It's crowded, isn't it? I told my niece..." He stopped, froze, stared. "Sarah?" he said. "Sarah Maxwell?"

The room spun in a kaleidoscope of color. For a moment Sarah thought she might faint. The room righted itself. She tried to speak and was afraid to.

"Sarah?" he said again. "It is you, isn't it?"

She took a deep breath. "Hello, Andres. It's nice to see you again. I didn't think you ever came to these affairs."

"I don't. But my niece is in the program this year. Mother would have brought her but she hasn't been feeling well."

"Oh? I'm sorry." Fifteen years, Sarah thought, and I'd have known him anywhere. He's just as tall as I remembered, just as ruggedly handsome. The thick black hair was threaded with silver at the temples now, but that seemed to make him even more attractive.

It's funny, she thought, even as she forced herself to chat with him, there's so much I still remember. The broadness of his shoulders, the strength of his hands, the cleft in his chin that saves his face from harshness.

"How's your father?" she asked.

"He died ten years ago, Sarah."

"I'm so sorry." Without thinking she touched his hand. "I liked him a lot. He was so kind to me, so courtly." A fleeting smile touched her lips. "He fixed me my first taco. I'd never tasted anything that hot before. I loved it."

"I'll never forget that first night at dinner when mother served you Chicken Pipián. You turned almost as green as the sauce when you saw it, but you ate every bite."

"I loved it," Sarah said with a laugh.

"You're here as a chaperone?"

"Yes." She took a steadying breath. "My son is part of the group."

"That answers my next question." One dark brow rose. "I was about to ask if you were married."

"Widowed. I ... I lost my husband before Richard was born. My name is Carlson now." She looked around for Rachel Carney, for anyone she knew so that she could make an excuse to walk away. But before she could think of a reason she saw Richard coming toward her through the crowd, a pretty young girl at his side.

"Mother..." His face was flushed with pleasure. "Mother, this is Silvia. We're going to take some of the same classes together. She's invited us to brunch on Sunday. It's all right, isn't it? I told her I was sure it was. Her uncle owns a ranch and he raises bulls. She said it would be all right with him and—"

"Slow down, young man," Andres said with a laugh. "It's perfectly all right with her uncle. He'd be delighted to have you and your mother join him for Sunday brunch."

The girl with Richard gave a delighted peal of laughter. "This is wonderful, Uncle Andres," she said. "I had no idea the lady you were talking to was Richard's mother." She held her hand out to Sarah. "I'm Silvia Navarro, señora. You will come on Sunday, won't you?"

For a moment Sarah could only stare at the girl. "I ... I'm afraid we have something else planned for Sunday," she managed to say.

"Mom!" Richard looked stunned. "I've never been on a ranch before. I want to go." He swallowed hard. "Please, Mom."

"Yes, please," Silvia entreated.

"Your mother is ill," Sarah protested as she turned to Andres. "It would inconvenience her."

"Nonsense, Sarah. Mother will be delighted to see you again." He smiled at Richard. "Your mother spent a month at El Camichín a long time ago. It's going to be a little like history repeating itself to have her there again, especially with her son. How old are you, Richard?"

"Almost fifteen. Mom told me she'd spent a summer at a ranch near Guadalajara but when Silvia told me about your ranch I had no idea it would be the same one. I can't wait to see it."

"Good. I'll pick you up at ten. Be sure to wear jeans in case you and Silvia want to go riding."

"I will, Mr. Navarro. Thanks a lot."

"Richard, Señora Navarro is ill," Sarah said nervously. "I think it would be better if we waited a bit. Perhaps we'll find time before we leave."

"But, Mom..."

"A visit from you would do a lot for mother," Andres insisted. "She's talked about you often through the years, Sarah. I know she'll want to see you."

Sarah clenched her hands. "We're here with other students, Andres. I'm one of the chaperones and I...I really don't think Richard and I can make plans for Sunday."

"Mother!" Richard only called her that when he was upset. "It's only for one day. Miss Carney can get along okay. The kids aren't *kids*, they don't need somebody to take care of them every minute."

"I know, dear, but—"

"Please, Mom."

Sarah took a deep breath. She looked from Andres to Richard and knew that she'd been defeated. "All right," she said.

Andres smiled at Richard. "It's a date," he said. "Ten o'clock Sunday." He acknowledged Richard's thanks and smiled as he watched the boy and Silvia thread their way back through the crowd. "He's a nice boy," he told Sarah. "But he doesn't have your coloring, does he? Was his father Latin?"

"No," she said, too quickly. Then trying to recover added, "Yes. I . . . I mean he was Portuguese."

"With a name like Carlson?"

"The family shortened it."

"He's a handsome boy. You must be proud of him, Sarah. Would you like a glass of wine?" He took her arm and led her toward a table in the far corner, away from the mariachis.

Sarah wanted to get away from him. She wanted to get Richard and take the first plane back to Miami. Carlos would be at the ranch, with his wife, Maria Escobar. She couldn't face him. She couldn't let him see Richard.

She looked out at the dancing couples and saw Richard dancing with Silvia. Dear God, she thought with something near panic, he's dancing with his half sister. Then, because she had to be sure she said, "Silvia is Carlos's daughter?"

Andres nodded. "She's fourteen."

"She's a very pretty girl." Sarah took the glass of wine he offered and holding it with both hands asked, "How is Carlos?"

She saw his eyes change. "Carlos is dead," he said. "He and Maria were killed in a car crash six years ago."

Sarah stood perfectly still. She thought of how Carlos had looked the night of his twenty-first birthday. He'd been so young, so handsome, so sure of himself. He'd had his whole life before him, and now he was dead. She thought of Maria Escobar too, of her beauty and fragility, and felt tears sting her eyes. "I'm sorry," she said. "I'm so sorry."

"It was hard on Mother. Having Silvia helped her get through. It helped me too because I became a surrogate father." He took a sip of his wine and looking at Sarah over the rim of the glass said, "I don't suppose you'd care to dance."

"No, I . . . no, thank you."

"Oh, come on. Let's show these kids what it's like to dance together." He took the wineglass from Sarah's hand and led her out onto the floor.

Andres had thought of her often during the past fifteen years. Now as he held her in his arms it seemed to him that she'd changed very little. She must be thirty-two or three. Her hair was still golden-blond and her wide amber eyes still sparkled with specks of pure gold. But there was a look of elegance about her now, a look of confidence she hadn't possessed fifteen years ago.

He still remembered how she had looked, waiting in the lobby of the Hotel Fénix, the first time he'd seen her. He didn't know what he'd expected, but Sarah wasn't anything like he'd imagined she would be.

"What a great-looking girl," Carlos had told him the night before when he'd come in from the reception. "She's a knockout, big brother. She's got this soft creamy skin, blond hair down to her shoulders..." Carlos had rolled his eyes. "I can't wait to find out if she's creamy smooth all over."

"Dammit, Carlos, you keep your hands off this little gringa or I'll have Mother send her to a different family."

"There aren't any other families." Carlos grinned. "Our Miss Maxwell was apparently the last one of her group to register. And we were the last family on the list. We're stuck with her, Andres. I guess we'll just have to make the best of it."

"Stay away from her," Andres said. "That's an order."

He'd gone to the hotel to pick her up the next day, expecting to find what? Somebody who chewed gum and wore a tight red sweater over a size forty-two bust? Instead he'd found Sarah, looking rather prim in a plain blue suit, stockings and clean white pumps. He thought of Carlos and suddenly he'd wanted to say, "You'll be no match for my brother. Go back to wherever you came from while you have a chance."

That's what a part of him wanted to do. The other part of him wanted to take her hand and lead her to some quiet place where they could be alone.

Of course, Andres hadn't done either of those things. Instead he'd kept his eye on her. After Carlos's birthday party he'd been afraid that Carlos might get too close to her and ruin the arrangements that had been made with the Escobars, so he'd taken Sarah up into the hills. He'd told her that Carlos was destined to carry on the Navarro name, that his sons and his son's sons would be on this Navarro land forever. But Carlos and Maria had no sons. Would things have been different, Andres wondered now, if Carlos had married Sarah?

For a moment Andres rested his face against her fair hair. He breathed in the scent of her, the scent of sunlight and of silk whispering against a woman's skin—Sarah's skin.

He remembered the way she had looked at him that day on the hill overlooking El Camichín. As long as he lived he'd never forget the shock on her face, the shame and a bottomless sorrow that had shaken him right down to his riding boots. He hadn't been able to help himself. He had to take her in his arms and comfort her.

Sarah had felt so small and vulnerable in his arms. He'd wanted to tell her that he was sorry he'd hurt her. Instead he'd kissed her.

Now, after all these years, holding Sarah in his arms this way, he remembered.

His arms tightened around her. "Why didn't you tell me you were leaving El Camichín?" he asked. "You told Mother you were homesick, but that wasn't it, was it? You left because I'd hurt you. Because you were in love with Carlos and I told you about his and Maria's engagement."

"No." Sarah's face was shadow pale. "No, Andres, I...I *was* homesick. I'd never been away before. I..." She looked up at him. "It was time to go home," she said.

The music stopped. Still Andres stood close to her, his gaze resting on her face.

From somewhere a voice said, "Party's over, friends. See you in school bright and early Monday morning."

Andres took Sarah's hand. "Until Sunday," he said.

Chapter Five

Sunday dawned bright and clear.

"I can't believe that Silvia's family was your host family," Richard said as they waited in the hotel lobby. "She's a great-looking girl, isn't she, Mom? What was her father like? Was he the same age you were?"

"No, he was a little older."

"Did he look like Silvia's uncle? Mr. Navarro's a pretty good-looking guy, for his age I mean. What's the ranch like?"

Before Sarah could answer a dark-blue car pulled up in front of the hotel and Silvia jumped out.

"Good morning, Mrs. Carlson," she said politely. "Hi, Rico. All ready to go?"

"Rico?" Richard asked with a pleased smile.

"That's what I'm going to call you. Okay?"

"Okay!" he said enthusiastically as he followed her out to the car where Andres waited.

"Buenos días," Andres said. "Glad you remembered to wear jeans, Richard."

"Rico." Silvia's voice was firm. "We're going to call him Rico, Uncle Andres."

"Fine, that suits him." He smiled at Sarah and as he helped her into the car said, "You look like summer."

"Thank you." She avoided his gaze as she smoothed the skirt of her jonquil-yellow dress. "Are you sure your mother's well enough for company?"

"She felt better the minute she knew you were coming. She's looking forward to seeing you, Sarah, and to meeting Richard." He smiled at the two young people in the back seat. "Sorry—Rico."

When he merged with the traffic he looked into his rearview mirror. "Ever seen a bullfight?" he asked Richard. "There's going to be a good one in two weeks. I thought maybe you and your mother would like to go."

"Would we! That'd be great, Señor Navarro."

Sarah glanced at Andres. Why had he taken a sudden interest in Richard? And in her? He hadn't liked her very much when he'd known her fifteen years ago. Why did he feel he had to entertain her and her son now?

She and Andres had little to say on the way to the ranch. But Richard and Silvia talked and laughed enough for the four of them. That disquieted Sarah. She didn't want any kind of a relationship to develop between the two young people. She'd do anything she must to prevent it.

When Andres turned off the highway onto the road leading to El Camichín, Sarah looked back at Richard and said, "We're almost there."

They came to the rise that looked down on the ranch and Andres stopped, as he had that first day so long ago. "There it is," he said to Richard. "El Camichín."

"It's fantastic." Richard's voice was respectful. "Is all of it yours?"

"Yes, it's all Navarro land." A smile twitched at the corners of Andres's mouth. "The first time I brought your mother here she saw the bulls and thought they were cows."

"Mom!" Richard's hand closed over her shoulder and he laughed. "How could you?"

"I was raised in the city," Sarah said. "What did I know?"

"Could I get out for a minute?" Richard asked.

"Sure, go ahead," Andres said. When Richard and Silvia scrambled out he came around to Sarah's door and took her hand to help her out of the car.

So much is the same, Sarah thought. The golden fields were still dotted with crimson poppies and hollyhocks. Birds still wheeled and darted into the wild mustard grass. With a sigh she turned to speak to Richard and stopped. There was an expression on his face she'd never seen before, a look of such wonder and longing that for a moment Sarah wanted to reach out and touch him. Oh please, she thought. Please don't look like that.

She glanced quickly at Andres and saw that he, too, was watching Richard. He looked as though he was about to speak when Silvia said, "Let's go, Rico. I can't wait to show you the ranch."

The years had been kind to Teresa Navarro, but it was obvious that she wasn't well. She greeted Sarah warmly and said, "My dear, you've grown into a perfectly beautiful woman. How lovely you look and how nice it is to see you again."

"You too, Doña Teresa." Sarah kissed the older woman's cheek. "I'd like you to meet my son, Richard. Richard, this is Señora Navarro."

"Ma'am." He shook her hand. "It's a pleasure to meet you."

"Call him Rico, Grandmother," Silvia said. "That's what I'm going to call him. Is it all right if I show him the stable now?"

"But we must eat first."

"Just the stable, Grandmother. I promise we'll come right back. I can show him the rest of the ranch after brunch."

"All right, Silvia. But ten minutes only." Teresa smiled as Silvia grabbed Richard's hand and disappeared around the side of the house. "Children," she said. "I sometimes wonder if I was ever that young."

"Would you like a sherry, Mother? How about you, Sarah?"

"Yes, please, Andres." His mother took Sarah's arm. "Come, my dear. We're eating out on the patio. Let's enjoy our sherry there, shall we?"

Fifteen years have passed, Sarah thought as she helped Teresa Navarro out to the patio. But the house is the same, and here in the patio it's as though the same flowers are still blooming. Any moment I expect Carlos to come dashing out, charming and gay and young, almost unable to contain his joy at just being alive.

"I was so sorry to hear about Carlos," Sarah said when she and Teresa were seated. "And his wife. That must have been terrible for you."

"It was, Sarah." A look of intense pain crossed the older woman's face. "I don't think I'll ever get over it. Silvia was eight years old when Carlos and Maria were killed. I couldn't just sit back and mourn, I had to care for her, to try to help her understand what had happened." She patted Sarah's hand. "Carlos was so fond of you, my dear. He pouted for days after you left." She smiled as Andres approached with a silver tray, accepted her glass of sherry and said, "But summer romances fade when summer ends, don't they?"

"That sounds profound," Andres said. "What's it supposed to mean?"

"Sarah and I were speaking of Carlos. I was telling her that Carlos was most unhappy when she left us so suddenly."

"Summer had ended," Sarah said. "It was time to go home."

It was pleasant on the sunlit patio. When Richard and Silvia returned brunch was served. For the first time in his life Richard tasted *machaca*, *huevos rancheros*, corn tortillas hot off the *comal*, and the hot sauce that Sarah remembered so well.

"This is wonderful," Richard said as he scooped up the last bit of *huevos rancheros* on his plate with a piece of tortilla. "Sure isn't like Taco Bell, is it, Mom?"

"Not exactly." Sarah smiled as she settled back in her chair. "I'd almost forgotten how good a cook you are, Doña Teresa."

"All I do now is supervise I'm afraid."

"But that's the most important part, *mamá*." Andres covered his mother's hand with his. "You look tired, dear. Would you like to rest for a bit?"

"Yes, I believe I would if Sarah will excuse me." She allowed Andres to help her up, then turning to Sarah said, "You'll be here for supper of course." And before Sarah could answer Teresa turned to Richard and said, "Have you ever had *quesadillas*?"

"I don't think so."

"*Bien*, that's what we'll have for dinner then. *Quesadillas* and *chiles rellenos*. Now run along. Be sure to make Silvia show you everything."

"Mother's really enjoying Richard," Andres told Sarah when they were alone. "I'm afraid she forced that dinner invitation. I hope you didn't have any plans."

"No, it's all right." This time, Sarah told herself, but I'll make sure it doesn't happen again.

"Rico's a nice boy," Andres said, breaking in on her thoughts. "You've done a wonderful job with him, Sarah."

"Thank you."

"Ever thought about remarrying?"

"No," she said quickly. "Richard and I are quite happy."

"But he'll be off to the university in a few years. You'll be alone then."

"It doesn't matter. I have my job. And wherever he goes, Richard and I will always be close."

"Yes, I'm sure you will." Andres looked out toward the stable. "There they go," he said. "I knew Silvia would get him on a horse. They've really taken to each other, haven't they? Maybe it's a good thing you're only going to be here for three weeks; Silvia's much too young to be interested in a boy."

"Especially an American boy. We all know how promiscuous young people are in the United States."

"Sarah, I didn't mean—"

"I know what you meant." She turned away, as furious with herself as she was with him. Oh God, why had she let him talk her into coming here today? First it was brunch, then dinner, next a bullfight. She couldn't allow Richard to become involved with the Navarro family. It was too dangerous.

She felt Andres's hand on her arm. "We need to talk, Sarah," he said. "Let's go for a walk." Before she could resist he took her hand and led her out of the patio.

For a long time they didn't speak, but Andres kept Sarah's hand in his until they came to a fenced-in pasture. When he let her go she said, "I'm sorry, Andres, for what I said back there. I didn't mean to. It just came out."

"You've never forgotten, have you?" He looked out across the distant field. "I've been sorry for a long time about what I said to you that last day, Sarah. It's fifteen years too late, but I hope you'll accept my apology."

Sarah looked at him, too surprised to speak.

"I wrote to you a hundred times," Andres said. "Once I even mailed the letter. But it came back with 'Not Here' scrawled across it."

"I left Chicago after high school," she said. "I went to live with my aunt in Miami."

"And your parents chose not to forward your mail."

"Apparently."

Andres leaned his elbows on the fence and looked out over the meadow and the pasture where the bulls grazed. He'd told Sarah the truth, he *had* thought about her often through the intervening years. When he had written it had been to apologize for his harshness that day on the hill.

He'd been shocked when he came back to the house from Jocotepec the next day to find Sarah gone and Carlos livid with anger.

"It's all for the best," Andres had told his younger brother. "You're going to marry Maria Escobar. You had no business chasing after Sarah, no matter how willing she was."

Carlos had turned on him in fury. "Damn you," he'd shouted. "You don't know anything about Sarah."

I held her in my arms, Andres almost said. I held her and maybe she was damn good at pretending, but I could have sworn she answered my kiss with enough enthusiasm to start a brush fire.

But even as Andres had thought the words he felt a flush of shame, because it hadn't been like that. Sarah had been as surprised as he was by the sudden desire that flamed between them. Her body had trembled against his and for a moment she'd fought to break free. He'd heard her gasp of surprise, the whisper of protest, and it hadn't mattered. All that had mattered was that at last Sarah was in his arms. Then her lips softened under his and her arms crept up around his neck. He had never wanted a woman as much as he'd wanted Sarah.

But he'd let her go. The next day she had fled back to her own country. Because he felt guilty and ashamed he'd said to his brother, "I saw the way you

and Sarah acted around each other. I know that school
lets out at three o'clock and it takes exactly twenty
minutes from there to the ranch. I know too that most
afternoons you and Sarah didn't show up here until
after five."

He'd raised one mocking eyebrow. "It was obvious
she wasn't inexperienced, Carlos. I..." He still remembered how painful it had been to say what he had
to say. But he had to know. "I suspect you've bedded
her a number of times this summer and I don't blame
you. But don't let it go to your head, Carlos, she—"

Carlos hit him. As Andres stumbled back, too
stunned to speak, Carlos said, "You're right. I did bed
her. *Once*, Andres. Only once. It was the night of my
birthday. I'd had too much wine and I broke into her
room through the French doors."

"You *broke* in?"

"Yes, dammit." Carlos had flushed. "Sarah was
scared and she tried to make me leave. I thought she
was teasing, that she wanted to just as much as I did."
He ran a frantic hand through his dark hair. "Oh
hell," he said, "I don't know what I thought. All I
knew was how badly I wanted her and that by God I
was going to have her. I...I guess I made her do it."
Carlos looked at his brother. "She was a virgin," he
said. "This girl that you thought was so experienced
had never been with a man before, Andres."

The two brothers had stared at each other. Then,
without speaking, Andres had turned away. He'd
taken a horse from the stable and ridden hell-bent up

into the hills. When at last he reined in the winded horse he went to stand on the rocks where he'd stood with Sarah only a few days before. He remembered that her face had looked sick with shame and he knew it had been he who'd shamed her.

He turned to her now and saw that she was looking out toward the mountains. A breeze ruffled her short honey-colored hair and she raised an impatient hand to sweep it out of her eyes. Suddenly Andres wanted to touch her. He wanted to say, I'm sorry, Sarah, for so many things. I want to begin again. I want to pretend that this is your first day at El Camichín. I want to hold you in my arms.

Instead he talked of the changes he'd made on the ranch since his father's death and of the new stallion he'd bought last week. After a while he took Sarah's hand and they went back to the house.

Chapter Six

A *tienta*?'' Richard asked that night at dinner. ''What's that?''

''It's when we test cows for bravery,'' Andres said. ''If they're brave then they're used in breeding. We also test the *beceros*—the young bulls—to find the bravest among them. This is the way we select the bulls who will face a matador in the bullring two years from now.''

Andres leaned forward in his chair. ''You see, Rico, the word 'bull' has a special connotation in the Mexican and the Spanish mind. It doesn't mean just the male of the cow, it means a fighting animal, an animal that's a million years removed from the Hereford or the Jersey, or even the Texas longhorn. A fighting bull isn't savage, he's brave. The bulls here on El Camichín are the product of two hundred years of selective breeding.''

Richard's eyes never left Andres's face. "I watched the bulls through the fence today,'' he said. "I can't imagine what it would be like to see them in the ring.''

"It's one of the most exciting spectacles in the world,'' Teresa Navarro said slowly. "A tragic ballet in which a prime specimen of man faces a prime specimen of animal in a life-and-death struggle. You may not like it when you see your first bullfight, my boy, but you'll never forget it.''

"I'd like it,'' Richard said.

"A *tienta* isn't a bullfight,'' Silvia broke in, "but it'll give you a little taste of what the real thing is like.'' Her face was alive with excitement. She was a pretty girl, and even at fourteen there was a hint of the beauty she'd be when she was grown. Her skin, tanned by the sun and by the blood of her ancestors, was flawless. She had her father's features but her black-velvet eyes were just like her mother's.

"Next Sunday at our *tienta* Uncle Andres and some other men, maybe even a couple of matadors, will take the cape to test the *beceras*, the young cows,'' Silvia said. "When they get a really good cow they can make some nice passes, Rico. It's a lot of fun and it's exciting.'' She looked across the table at Andres and said, "We can invite Rico and his mother, can't we, *Tío*?''

"Only if I can get a word in,'' Andres said. He smiled at Richard. "How would you and your mother like to spend next weekend with us? I could use an extra man at the *tienta*."

For a moment Richard looked too startled to speak. Then his face broke into a broad smile. "I could help?"

"I don't see why not. In spite of what Silvia says, the testing of the cows is a serious business. I need all the help I can get."

Sarah looked at her son, then at Andres, trying to fight her anger and her rising panic. What did Andres think he was doing? Why had he taken such a sudden interest in Richard? This had to be stopped before it went any further.

"I'm afraid we can't," she said firmly. "The school is planning a trip to the falls at Juanacatlán next weekend and—"

"Mother!" Richard looked horrified. "I don't care anything about a dumb trip to some dumb falls. I want to be here at the ranch. When am I ever going to get a chance to see a *tienta* again?"

"I hope you'll reconsider," Teresa said. "It's going to be a special weekend, Sarah. We're having an old-fashioned fiesta on Saturday night, with dinner, music and dancing. It's typically Mexican and I'm sure Rico would enjoy it. I know you would too."

"But I—" Sarah tried to say.

"Please, Señora Carlson," Silvia begged. "It'll be nice for you too, coming back I mean. It'll be like old times."

Like old times. Sarah's eyes met Andres's across the table.

"Mom, please." Richard's young voice was desperate. "I don't want to go to the falls, I want to come here. This ... the ranch, it isn't like anything I've ever seen. It's wonderful here. I love it more than any place I've ever been. I don't care if I ever see a city again. I could spend the rest of my life right here."

Sarah clenched her hands together in her lap. She wanted to take Richard's hand and run away, as far as she could get from El Camichín. Far away from these people, his grandmother, his uncle, his half sister.

She looked around the table and knew, that at least for now, she had no choice except to give in. There were four of them to only one of her. Four Navarros against one lone gringa.

Sarah had brought one fairly modest evening dress with her, a simple strapless black silk that she knew wouldn't do for the Navarros' party. On Friday, while Richard was in school, she went to the Mercado Libertad, Guadalajara's huge and colorful central market. After walking up and down in front of the countless stalls for more than an hour, she bought an ankle-length rose-pink dress that was embroidered around the bodice and the edge of the skirt in deeper shades of rose. It was worn off the shoulder and fell to Sarah's ankles in wide rows of ruffles. It was a party dress; a typically Mexican dress.

"Have fun," Rachel Carney told her that Friday night. "Don't worry about us. Some of the host families are going along on the trip to the falls. We'll have plenty of chaperones."

El Camichín was alive with excitement when Sarah and Richard arrived that Saturday afternoon.

"I've got the horses saddled," Silvia told Richard. "We've got time for a ride before we have to dress."

He handed his bag to Sarah. "It's okay, isn't it, Mom?"

"Yes, it's okay." Sarah had been quiet and withdrawn all week. She'd known that Richard thought she was angry with him for being so insistent about coming to the ranch. But she wasn't angry, at least not at Richard. Now, impulsively, Sarah kissed his cheek and said, "Have a good time, sweetie. Just don't forget to come back."

"I won't." He looked relieved. "See you later."

"He's such a nice boy," Teresa said with a smile. "He reminds me of..." A look of pain crossed her face. Then, as though mentally shaking herself she said, "Come along, Sarah, let me take you to your room."

It was the same room Sarah had had fifteen years ago.

"I thought you might enjoy being in here again," Teresa said as Sarah looked around.

The fine old furniture was the same, only the carpet and the curtains had been changed. A bowl of summer-fresh daisies adorned the dresser.

"Silvia picked them." The older woman smiled. "She's a dear child, Sarah. The joy of my life. It's been lonely here for her. Andres is busy with the ranch and I'm so much older. Except for school, Silvia isn't around young people. I'm sorry that you and Rico are going to be in Guadalajara for such a short time. I wish the two of you could stay with us for a while."

"I'm sure Richard wishes the same thing." Sarah smiled.

"It's strange, but in so many ways Rico reminds me of Carlos at that age. He has the same excitement, the same enthusiasm for life that Carlos had." She turned away and covering her eyes said, "I do miss him so."

"I know you do." Sarah put her arms around Teresa's shoulders, something she'd never have dared to do fifteen years ago. But when Teresa left Sarah sank down on the bed and leaning her face against the wood-grained bedpost closed her eyes.

This is a nightmare, she thought. Any minute I'll wake up and find myself back in my own bedroom in Miami, listening to the stereo blasting from Richard's room. Dear Lord, Sarah asked herself, what am I doing here? Of all the places in the world she didn't want to be it was here in the Navarro home. A moment ago, when Teresa said that Richard reminded her of Carlos, she'd thought she was going to be physically ill.

Slipping out of her shoes, Sarah lay across the bed and stared up at the ceiling. This was the bed where Richard had been conceived, and even now she remembered her fear and her humiliation. Sarah lay there for a long time and slowly all of the hate and resentment she'd felt for Carlos all these years faded into the past. She forgave him and she forgave herself.

Two hours later, just as she pulled the rose-pink dress over her head, there was a knock on the door. When Sarah opened it one of the maids handed her a tissue-wrapped gardenia.

"Thank you," Sarah murmured. She closed the door and stared down at the perfect flower. Then she raised it to her face and felt the dewy freshness of it against her skin before she pinned it in her hair.

The patio was already filled with people by the time Sarah stepped out into the soft night. Lanterns were strung on overhanging trees, candles burned in wall sconces. A half moon shone down from a cloudless sky. Sarah closed her eyes, listening to the mariachis play a Mexican waltz.

"Would you care to dance?" Andres had said so long ago. She'd been afraid of him then, but there'd been an excitement in her fear, and something—

"Would you care to dance?"

Sarah opened her eyes and looked at Andres. "Thank you for the gardenia," she said. "For both of the gardenias."

His lips quirked with a smile. "You're doubly welcome." His eyes met hers. "You're beautiful tonight, Sarah."

"Thank you." She felt the beat of pulse in her throat when he took her hand and led her to where the other guests were dancing.

For several minutes Andres didn't speak. Then he said, "I still remember the first time we danced. I had all kinds of preconceived ideas about you. I thought you'd been around, that you'd known many young men and that you'd probably been to dozens of dances. Then I felt you tremble and I knew you weren't as experienced as I'd thought. It made me feel protective, Sarah. It made me feel..." His arms tightened around her and he brought her hand up and tucked it against his chest.

Sarah could feel the warmth of his skin through his white ruffled shirt, the pressure of his hand against her back. Oh don't, she thought. Don't hold me like this, Andres. She looked into his cave-black eyes, then away. "Richard..." She took a steadying breath and started again. "Richard seems to be having a good time. I'm surprised to see him dancing. For the last two years he's pretended to hate it."

"Silvia can be pretty persuasive." Andres chuckled. "He looks as though he's enjoying it now." He smiled at Sarah. "I hope you are too."

"Of course. But I...I really must go speak to your mother, Andres. Please excuse me."

For the rest of the evening Sarah managed to avoid being alone with Andres. She sat next to Teresa when dinner was served at ten. The older woman looked beautiful tonight, dressed in black lace, her silver hair swept up, diamonds sparkling in her ears.

"We never have a fiesta," Teresa said, "that I don't remember Carlos's twenty-first birthday. You were here then, Sarah. Do you remember the party?"

"Of course I remember." Sarah forced a smile.

"I watched the two of you that night. I have to admit that I was afraid that Carlos was falling in love with you and I knew that it would have been an impossible match. Federico told me not to worry. He said summer romances come and go as swiftly as the seasons. He was right of course. Carlos married Maria and you went back to your own country, found a young man, married him and had your son. So you see how foolish I was to worry. Everything turned out all right, didn't it?"

Sarah waited a moment before replying. "Yes," she said finally. "Everything turned out all right, Doña Teresa."

"I'm so sorry though that you lost your husband. It must have been terrible for you, Sarah. You were what...eighteen when Rico was born? Thank God you had the support of your family."

"Of my aunt." For the first time Sarah allowed a note of bitterness to creep into her voice. She hesitated, then said, "I think I'd better see what that young son of mine is up to."

What Richard was up to was the best evening of his life. Ten of his and Silvia's friends from school had been invited to tonight's party, but not to the Sunday *tienta.* They laughed, danced, and drank great quantities of cola with the Mexican appetizers. When for a moment Richard was alone with Sarah he said, "Thanks for letting us come this weekend, Mom." He looked around him. "I can't believe people live like this. It's great, isn't it? I like the food and the music... I like everything. Silvia's a great girl, isn't she? Mr. Navarro's a really terrific guy and Grandmother Teresa's a doll."

"She's not your grandmother," Sarah said, more sharply than she intended.

"Yeah, but she asked me to call her that anyway. She's nice, Mom. I like her a lot. She's not like your..." He blushed. "I'm sorry, Mom."

"It's all right, Richard."

He'd only seen Sarah's parents on special occasions, once at a funeral for her father's mother, and once when her mother had been ill and Sarah had gone to take care of her for two weeks. There had never been any warmth between her parents and Richard. As far as they were concerned he was an outsider, a bastard child who had no place in their family.

"I can't wait till tomorrow," Richard said. "Silvia told me that sometimes Uncle Andres lets one or two of the guests have a turn with the cape. Do you think he'd let me try, Mom? Maybe if you ask him..."

"I have no intention of asking him. And don't you even think about stepping into that bullring."

He was about to reply when Silvia appeared. "I want Rico to meet somebody, Señora Carlson. It's

Jaime Toscano, Rico, a *numero uno* matador. He just got here. He's going to be at the *tienta* tomorrow. Would you like to meet him?''

"Would I!''

"Go ahead,'' Sarah said with a smile. She stood watching the dancers for a few moments, then moved to the central fountain, banked now with dozens of pots of flowering azaleas. Tonight and tomorrow, she thought as she sat down. Then it will be over. I'll make sure Richard keeps busy this next week, and I'll have plans for next weekend. Then it will be time for us to leave Guadalajara. Once Richard's home he'll forget all about this.

"A peso for your thoughts,'' Andres said. He handed Sarah a glass of white wine. "It's a good party. Are you having fun?''

"Yes, thanks.'' She took a sip of the wine.

He sat next to her. "Tell me about yourself, Sarah. What do you do?''

"I work for an import-export company in Miami. We deal mostly with South American companies.''

"That's why your Spanish is so good. Do you like what you do?''

Sarah nodded. "I've been with the same company for a long time.''

"What about your social life?''

"I'm too busy with my job and Richard to do much socializing. I have dinner with friends occasionally.''

"Men friends?''

Sarah looked at Andres over the edge of her glass. "Sometimes."

"You're an attractive woman. I'm surprised you haven't remarried. You must have had a lot of opportunities these past fifteen years."

"None that I took seriously."

"I see." Andres took her hand and drawing her to her feet said, "I'd like to dance with you again."

The music was a rumba, the song "Begin the Beguine." Andres's arms tightened, drawing Sarah closer as they moved to the slow, sensuous rhythm. His chin brushed her honey-blond hair, he felt the cool, fragrant gardenia against his cheek. She's so light in my arms, he thought. I can feel the fragility of her bones through her dress. Her hand, tucked against my chest, is so small, so warm. If I uncurled my fingers I could brush the pale rise of her breasts.

Sarah looked up at him. In the flickering light of the lanterns her amber eyes turned to pure gold. Andres felt his breath catch in his throat, and a flicker of fire turn into a blaze somewhere inside him. His arms tightened around her; he knew he'd wanted her for fifteen years. He had to be alone with her. He had to touch her. Some day soon he knew he had to lie with her, make love to her, and hear her cry his name in the silent darkness of the night.

He stopped dancing. He looked down at her, his face harsh with longing.

"Andres?" Sarah whispered his name. "What is it?"

"I...I've had too much wine. I need some air." He took Sarah's hand and led her away from the dancers, away from the house, down the path toward the distant trees.

Sarah could have broken away from him, but instead she let him lead her away from the music and the dancing, into the darkness. She was afraid but didn't know what it was she feared. She only knew that her heart beat hard against her ribs and that the touch of Andres's hand clasping hers was warm and strong.

When they reached the trees he veered to the left toward the meadow. He stopped, took a deep breath and said, "Thank you for coming with me, Sarah."

"What is it, Andres?"

"You know what it is, Sarah. I think we've both known since the moment I saw you a few nights ago at the reception. Maybe we even knew it fifteen years ago when we stood on that hill overlooking El Camichín." He moved closer and in a low voice said, "I've got to kiss you, Sarah. I've got to..."

She tried to speak but he stopped her words with his kiss. She could feel the barely restrained emotion in the tense hardness of his body. His arms went around her back, holding her so close she could barely breathe.

His mouth demanded surrender—a surrender Sarah wouldn't willingly give. She tried to break free but his arms were like steel bands that refused to release her. His mouth was insistent. She felt the warm moistness of his tongue against her lips and tried with every ounce of strength in her body to deny the flame that grew within her—tried and failed. Her lips softened against his and she yielded to the hands that urged her closer.

At last, with his lips still against hers, Andres said, "I've wanted to do that for a long time, Sarah. I've thought about you, wondered about you. When I saw you the other night at the reception I couldn't believe you were actually here in Guadalajara." He put his hands against her fair hair. "Little Sarah Maxwell," he murmured, "all grown-up into one of the loveliest women I've ever seen." He trailed his fingers down her bare shoulders. "You're so beautiful," he said in wonder. "So soft, so pale."

"Andres, please," Sarah whispered in a voice that trembled.

"Please what, Sarah? Please touch you like this?" He brushed the top of her breasts with his fingertips.

Sarah swayed against him. "Oh, don't," she pleaded. "Don't. I . . ." She tried to speak but his lips were warm against hers, more gently now, while his hands caressed her. Suddenly all of the slumbering desires that Sarah had held in check for so long simmered to the surface. Her skin burned, she felt as though the liquid fire in her veins had melted her bones. She pressed her body to his. Her hands crept up around the back of his neck and she threaded her fingers through his thick black hair.

"Sarah." Her name was a moan on his lips as he trailed a line of kisses down the side of her face to her throat, tasting her until he found the way to her breasts.

"No," she pleaded. "No, please. I..." With her last bit of willpower Sarah backed away.

Andres dropped his hands to his sides. He looked at Sarah and said, "I only meant to kiss you." He touched the side of her face. "There's so much I want to say to you, my dear. I want to tell you that I'm sorry for the way I treated you fifteen years ago. It took me a long time to know why I did."

Sarah looked up at him, her face shadowed by the clouds that moved to half cover the moon.

"You were too young for me then." He smiled. "You were too young for anybody. But I didn't think I could keep my hands off you so I told myself that you were just a little gringa who was only here for the summer. When I watched you and Carlos together..." He looked away from her. "It drove me crazy, Sarah. I wanted to kill him. I wanted to take you away and lock you in a room and make love to you. I wanted to hear you whisper my name and tell me that you desired me just as much as I desired you."

It was all Sarah could do not to move back into his arms and say, Do it now, Andres. Take me away now. Make love to me and I'll whisper your name. I'll do anything you want me to do. Only hold me, Andres, hold me.

Sarah didn't say the words because she knew there could never be anything between them. She'd made love to Andres's brother; she'd borne his child. If

Andres had been the first . . . but he hadn't been. Now he never could be.

"I want to begin again, Sarah," Andres said in a gentle voice. "I want to pretend we met for the first time at the reception the other night."

"Andres, I—"

He put a finger against her lips. "I want a chance to make up for all the harsh things I said to you that day on the hill." He drew her back into his arms. "I think I'm falling in love with you, Sarah."

Her fingers tightened on the lapels of his jacket. For a moment she rested her face against his shoulder, then she looked at him. "It's too late," she said. "It was too late for us a long time ago, Andres."

"But why? You know what we both feel. Don't deny us this, Sarah. Give us a chance to begin again."

"We can't, Andres. We just can't."

"Why? My God, Sarah, why?"

"I can't tell you." She moved out of his arms. "Richard and I are leaving Guadalajara in less than two weeks. We have our life, you have yours."

Sarah turned away so he wouldn't see the tears that welled in her eyes. "It's too late for us," she said again.

Chapter Seven

*P*uerta!'' Andres cried.

Two men threw open the wide door leading into the bullring and dashed to safety. A cow raced into the arena, sun glinting on the long, thin, razor-sharp horns.

"She's a beauty," Teresa whispered from her seat in the small grandstand. "Let's see what she does now, Sarah."

The young cow, eyes alert, raised her head, then raced toward the well-padded, blindfolded horse with such force that he was almost jarred off his feet as the picador jabbed his lance into her withers. Instead of backing off, the pic only infuriated her and she charged again.

"Muy bien," Teresa murmured as Andres ran into the bullring to lure the cow away from the horse with his magenta-and-yellow cape. But the cow only increased her attack.

"You see how she continues to charge?" Teresa's voice was excited. "A good cow will go after the pic again and again."

"But she's hurt," Sarah protested. "She's bleeding!"

"That will be attended to and the wounds will heal. Some day she'll bear brave bulls. Now watch Andres. He's changed the cape for the *muleta*, the small red cloth, so that he can learn more about her style."

Sarah watched the action below, almost breathless with excitement as Andres brought the animal close to his body. No one spoke. The only sounds were the rush of hooves against the earth, the bellows of the cows who waited in the corral, and the soft, "Aha!" as Andres called the animal closer.

He made a striking figure in his gray *traje corto*, the tight pants and short tight jacket that he wore with his Spanish boots. He must be forty-one or forty-two now, Sarah thought, but his body was just as slim and straight as it had been fifteen years ago. It was strange that he'd never married. Was it, she wondered, because he couldn't father children? Or was it that he'd never fallen in love?

As she watched him she thought of the previous night and how it had been there alone in the dark with him. Never before had she known such an over-whelming need to be possessed.

Sarah hadn't been a recluse these past years in Miami. She'd dated, once or twice seriously, but she'd never permitted herself to go all the way. There'd been a lot of reasons why she hadn't. One of course was the painful memory of the first and only time she'd made love. For a long while after that she'd wanted nothing to do with men. But as she matured she realized that sex needn't be the way it had been with her, and that when you loved a man everything was different. But that was just it, she hadn't fallen in love with anyone. So she'd held back. None of her relationships had gone beyond a few perfunctory kisses.

Until last night. What she had experienced with Andres had been beyond anything Sarah had ever dreamed of. She'd wanted him to make love to her. She'd wanted him to lay her down on the sweet-smelling meadow grass, to strip her and take her. Even now, watching him, her body grew warm with longing.

This thing between us is too volatile, Sarah thought, too dangerous. I've got to get away before something happens.

Sarah had seen Andres only briefly this morning when, accompanied by Richard, Silvia and Doña Teresa, she'd entered the family bullring. Richard had helped the elderly woman the few steps up to the seats before he and Silvia joined Andres and the other men behind the *barrera*, the heavy red wooden fence that enclosed the working area of the ring. Andres had looked up and come to where Sarah and his mother were sitting.

"Good morning, Mother, Sarah. It's a wonderful day for the *tienta*, isn't it? I'm glad you felt well enough to join us, Mother."

"I wouldn't have missed it for the world." Teresa smiled and nodding toward Richard said, "He's so excited he can barely stand it. It makes me feel good just to look at him. He reminds me so much of Carlos at that age." She turned to Sarah. "Perhaps that's why I'm so drawn to him."

"Rico certainly has taken to everything on the ranch," Andres said. "He loves it here, Sarah. I wish the two of you could stay for a while."

"Can't you, Sarah?" Teresa's face lit up. "It would be wonderful to have you and Rico here for the summer."

"That's impossible, Doña Teresa. I have my job to go back to."

"Would you consider letting Rico stay with us? We could ask him how he felt about it and if he—"

"No! He can't stay. He..." Sarah bit her bottom lip, sorry for her harshness. Then she covered Teresa's hand with her own. "It's kind of you to want him, but Richard has things ... activities in Miami that he's involved in."

"And do you have things you're involved in?" Andres asked. "Aside from your job, I mean?"

His gaze was intent on Sarah's face. "Have you?" he said softly.

Then from below someone had called, "Ready, Andres," and with one last look he'd turned away from her.

The morning passed swiftly. As cow after cow was tested each performance was carefully recorded in a ledger. Richard stood beside the man noting the performances, but after a while Andres sent him to help the man at the door leading into the ring.

When they broke for a light picnic lunch under the trees Richard rushed over to Sarah. His jeans were dusty and his face was dirty, but he looked happier than he'd ever been in his life.

"Have you ever seen anything like this before, Mom? Isn't it great? Isn't it just fantastic? Boy, what I wouldn't give to live here."

A knife twisted in Sarah's heart.

"Look at those mountains. And this land. It just goes on and on. Grandmother Teresa told me that all of this has been in the family for over two hundred years. Grandfathers and great-grandfathers, fathers and sons, from generation to generation, the same pastures, those same mountains." The clear dark eyes that looked out over the land were filled with longing. "It must be really great to belong to something like this," he said in a quiet voice.

"Yes, I suppose it is." Sarah touched his hand. "But Miami's a great place too." She tried to keep her voice light. "It's not too different from Mexico. We have the same blue skies, almost the same weather, and most of the people speak Spanish."

Richard looked at her and shook his head. "You don't understand," he said. "This isn't like any other place in the world. I wish..." He turned away from Sarah and gazed out at the distant mountains, a terrible hunger in his fine dark eyes.

After lunch, the formal business of the morning behind them, a few of the guests were allowed a turn with the *muleta*. Richard leaned against the *barrera*, watching the men make pass after pass.

Beside him Silvia said, "I'm bored, Rico. Let's go riding."

"Riding!" He looked at her as though she were crazy.

"We've been here almost all day and I'm tired of it." She lifted her heavy black hair off her neck. "It's so hot," she complained. "I want to be someplace cool and..."

But Richard wasn't paying any attention to her. His gaze was riveted on the man in the ring.

"Darn it, Rico," she snapped. "If you're so crazy about the bullring why don't you fight one of the cows?" He didn't bother to answer and with one last withering look Silvia turned away and went to sit in the grandstand next to her grandmother.

"Boys," she growled. "I want to go riding but Rico won't budge. He's mesmerized. All he wants to do is watch those darn cows."

"It's a new experience for him," Teresa said. "Let him alone, Silvia. You can go riding any time."

"But not with Rico, Grandmother. We'll be in school all week. Then there's just one more weekend and he'll be gone." She rested her chin in her hands as she watched the action below. "Rico's so much fun, Grandmother. I like him better than any of my other friends. I wish he could stay for a while."

"Yes, so do I, Silvia." Teresa looked at Sarah. "I wish you'd change your mind, dear," she said. "We'd love having you and Rico here for the summer."

"Thank you, Doña Teresa. But I'm afraid that's..." She stared down at the ring. One of the men had handed the red cloth to Richard.

"Look!" Silvia squealed. "Rico's going to give it a try."

"No!" Sarah started up out of her seat. "I've got to stop him. He can't—"

Teresa put her hand on Sarah's arm. "You mustn't go down there. It would embarrass the boy. He'll be all right, Sarah. Andres won't let anything happen to him. Besides, it's only a small animal."

"With sharp white horns." Sarah gripped the railing. She knew that Teresa was right; Richard would never forgive her if she ordered him out of the ring. But oh God, she was so afraid.

Richard ran into the ring, awkwardly extending his arms in front of him as the animal exploded into the small arena. It saw a flash of movement behind one of the *burladeros*, the wooden shield that extended slightly out in front of the opening in the *barrera*, and tore at it with razor-sharp horns.

Oh, please, Sarah silently prayed. Please be careful, Richard.

Richard stamped one foot. The animal charged with an amazing speed but Richard held his ground and moved the cloth slightly to the side of his body.

"*¡Olé!*" Silvia called. "*Bravo*, Rico!"

The young cow lowered her head and charged again, barely missing Richard's body.

Sarah rose. "No," she whispered. "Stop him."

Her voice was so low that Andres probably didn't hear her, but he looked up, saw her white face, and turning back to the arena said, "That's enough, Rico. I'll take her now."

"No! She's mine." Richard laughed. His face was flushed with excitement. "God, Andres, she's wonderful, isn't she?"

Andres grinned, then he sent a reassuring smile Sarah's way. Let the boy enjoy himself, he's having the time of his life, Andres thought as he turned back to the arena. He was pleased by Rico's enthusiasm. And he really wasn't bad, considering he'd never held a *muleta* before. He had a certain style, a grace of movement. He . . .

Andres froze. His mouth went dry. There was something about Rico, something in his stance, in the way he held the cloth, the particular angle of his face that reminded him of . . . My God, he looked just like

Carlos! Why hadn't he seen it before? He had the same facial structure, the same long lean body.

Andres wasn't aware that his face had gone white or that he gripped the side of the *barrera*, staring at the boy. He could have been watching Carlos. He ... Oh my God, he thought, I'm watching Carlos's son.

Andres whirled around, looking up at Sarah. His face was hard and angry with the knowledge.

Sarah stared at him, her eyes widening as she brought one hand to her mouth as though to hide a secret.

He knew then, he knew that it was true. For a moment he wanted to run up the stairs. He wanted to yank Sarah up out of her seat and shake her until he got the truth out of her. Damn her to hell, he'd get the truth, he'd—

A scream brought him back to reality. His head snapped back just as one sharp white horn caught Richard and lifted him high in the air. The boy hung there, suspended for one terrible moment before his body slammed to the earth.

Andres sprinted into the ring, the other men behind him frantically waving their capes as Andres picked Richard up and carried him out of the ring.

"Richard!" Sarah cried as she ran down the steps from the grandstand. "Oh, Richard!" She knelt beside him when Andres laid him down on the grass. She saw the blood on his leg.

"It's all right, Mom." He tried to sit up. "It's not so bad." He saw Silvia then, standing close to Sarah and said, "Hey, I was pretty good, wasn't I?"

"Your leg," Sarah moaned as she grasped Silvia's arm to steady herself. His leg had been ripped in an ugly jagged gash. She looked at Andres. "Do something," she begged.

"Juan," Andres called to one of the helpers. "Run to the house. Call Dr. Olsina and tell him to get over here right away."

"Sí, patrón," the man said as he dashed off.

Someone handed Andres a clean cloth and a roll of tape. He covered the wound, pressed hard to control the bleeding, then bound and taped it.

"That'll hold you until we get up to the house," he told Richard. Then he turned to Silvia. "Stop crying," he snapped. "Go and take care of your grandmother." He motioned Sarah out of the way as he picked Richard up. Then with her beside him and Richard in his arms, he ran toward the house.

Chapter Eight

By the time Andres cut away the leg of Richard's blue jeans and cleaned the skin around the wound, the doctor had arrived.

"I want my son taken to a hospital in Guadalajara," Sarah told him.

"Let me see him first, then we'll decide," the doctor said. "Perhaps a hospital is advisable, perhaps it isn't. It's better if you wait outside, señora."

"I'm okay, Mom," Richard said. "Don't make a fuss." His face was white and drawn with pain.

"I'll stay with him," Andres said. His face was as white as Richard's.

Sarah waited in the living room with Teresa and Silvia. The young girl was subdued, her face stained with tears. Teresa sat quietly, her eyes closed, fingering a rosary. At last, in a voice choked with pain, Teresa whispered, "You didn't want him to go into the ring, Sarah. It's my fault because I told you he would be all right."

"No, it wasn't your fault. The whole Mexican army couldn't have kept Richard out of the bullring." Sarah glanced down the silent corridor leading to the guest room where Richard was. "I wish the doctor would come out," she murmured.

"Olsina's a good man." Teresa opened her eyes. "He's handled hundreds of horn wounds. He knows what to do."

"I still think Richard should be in a hospital."

Teresa shook her head. "He's better off here where we can take care of him, Sarah. He—" She looked up as Dr. Olsina and Andres entered the corridor.

"How is he?" Sarah called as she jumped to her feet and ran to meet them.

"Your son's going to be all right, señora. But it was a nasty wound. He'll have to stay right where he is for at least fifteen days. After that it'll be another week or two before he's up and around."

"But we have to go back to Miami in ten days." Sarah stared at the doctor. "We can't stay here."

"I'm afraid you'll have to. Your boy's leg is badly torn up. He'll be good as new when it heals, but until it does he has to be immobile."

"Shouldn't he be in the hospital?"

"I'd rather he wasn't moved, Señora Carlson. Don't worry, your boy's going to be all right. I'll see him every day, at least for the first few days. Meantime I'm sure that between you and Doña Teresa and Silvia, Richard will have first-class care. Now why don't you go on in and see him? I've given him something for the pain so he's a little groggy. He'll likely have more pain when he wakes up. When he does you give him one of the little white pills I left on his dresser. The yellow pills are antibiotic and I've marked how often he's supposed to have one."

"Thank you, doctor." Sarah looked at Andres, then away. To Teresa she said, "I'm sorry. I know it's going to be a terrible inconvenience for you."

"An inconvenience? Even if Dr. Olsina had given his permission to remove Rico I'd have objected. Rico belongs here where we can take care of him."

"But three or four weeks—"

"More like a month and a half," the doctor said.

"A month and a half? But I—"

"Rico's waiting to see you," Andres said in a cold voice. "We can talk about this...about everything later."

Sarah was too chilled by the anger in his dark eyes to reply. Instead she turned away from him and hurried down the corridor to Richard's room.

His leg was propped up on a pillow, his eyes were heavy. "Hi, Mom. Did you hear the news? I've gotta stay here for a while. How about that?" He grinned sleepily up at her. "How about that?" he said again, and closed his eyes.

He awoke that night at ten in such pain that in spite of his efforts not to let on, he groaned. "My leg hurts, Mom," he said. "Gosh, it really hurts."

Sarah gave him one of the pills the doctor had left, then sat by him until he went back to sleep. Thank God he was going to be all right, she thought—but she wished they didn't have to stay here at the ranch.

With a sigh she rested her face against the side of the bed. Andres knows, she thought. He knows that Richard is Carlos's son. What am I going to do? Deny it? Tell Andres he's crazy? She closed her eyes. I'll lie if I have to, she thought. Richard's *my* son. He doesn't belong to anyone else.

When Richard's breathing evened Sarah slipped out of the room. She needed a cup of coffee to keep her awake and a thick robe to keep her warm.

The house was quiet and she thought everyone was asleep, but when she went into the kitchen she found Teresa at the kitchen table.

The older woman looked up as Sarah entered. Her face was tight with worry. "How's Richard?" she asked.

"He's asleep. I'm going to spend the night in his room."

"I'll have the servants bring in an extra bed."

"That's not necessary. The chaise will be fine." Sarah tried to smile reassuringly. "You should be asleep," she said.

"I can't sleep. I've been so worried about Richard. Now I'm worried about Silvia because she isn't in her room. I'd send Andres to find her but he's not here either. Would you mind taking a few minutes to look for her?"

"Of course not. Do you have any idea where she might be?"

"Down at the stable. That's where she always goes when she's upset. She's been so worried about Rico and I'm afraid she blames herself for the accident."

"But it wasn't her fault," Sarah objected. "It wasn't anybody's fault."

"Wasn't it?" The older woman's face looked sad. Then with a faint smile she said, "It's odd, isn't it, Sarah. We've known Rico for such a short time and yet we've all grown so fond of him. If he were any other young man I'd be concerned that Silvia's so taken with him. But theirs doesn't seem to be a boy-girl relationship, does it? It's more as if they were best friends. Now she's blaming herself because he's been hurt. I wish I could go to her but I—"

"I'll find her, Doña Teresa. You go to bed." Sarah stretched and rubbed the back of her neck. "I'll make sure Silvia's all right and safely tucked in bed."

"Thank you, my dear." Teresa took Sarah's hand. "I'm so sorry this happened, Sarah. I'd have given anything in the world if it hadn't."

Yes, so would I, Sarah thought as she went down the path to the stable. A month and a half! How could she and Richard stay here for that long? If he hadn't gone into the bullring, if he hadn't gotten hurt . . . But no, it wasn't Richard's fault. It was her fault for ever allowing him to come to Guadalajara.

Finally Sarah let herself think about Andres. He knew Carlos was Richard's father. She'd seen the shock of knowledge in his face this afternoon. Perhaps it had been the way Richard moved, or in the way he held the cape, but suddenly Andres had known. He'd looked at her . . . Sarah clenched her trembling hands together. Andres had looked at her with an anger that went beyond description.

The stable was lighted only by one ceiling lamp at the entrance. Sarah stood there for a moment, looking around her, sniffing the scent of hay and of horses, listening to the restless movement of the animals and one curious whinny of welcome.

"Silvia?"

There was no answer as Sarah peered into the first stall, then proceeded down the length of the stable, rubbing noses and scratching ears until she came to the last stall. She paused, then saw Silvia, back against the wall, head bent on her knees.

"Silvia?" she said again softly, then carefully entered the stall.

The girl raised a startled, tear-streaked face. "What . . . what do you want?" she whispered.

"Just to talk to you." Sarah sat on the straw beside her. "Richard's going to be all right," she said. "He'll have to stay in bed for a while but he's going to be fine."

"It was my fault."

"No, it wasn't. It wasn't anybody's fault." Sarah handed her a tissue.

"But I told Rico if he was so crazy about everything he should go into the ring. And he did and he got hurt and it's . . . it's my fault." Silvia buried her head against her knees again and began to sob.

Sarah put her arm around the girl and drew her close. After a few moments Sarah said, "Wild horses couldn't have kept Richard from going into the ring, Silvia. He's almost a man and he wanted to do what the other men were doing. I was so afraid that I wanted to rush right into the arena, grab him by the ear and haul him out of there."

"I wish you had." Silvia lifted her face and smiling through her tears said, "Wouldn't that have been a sight?"

"He'd never have forgiven me. All mothers want to protect their children, but maybe I'm overprotective because Richard's all I have. I have to remind myself every day that he's almost a man and that I can't smother him. But it's hard, Silvia."

"I guess it is." Silvia looked at Sarah curiously. "It must have been difficult, raising Rico alone, Mrs. Carlson. Maybe hard for him too, not having a father I mean."

"I'm sure it was." Sarah hesitated. "Do you suppose you could call me Sarah instead of Mrs. Carlson? I'd really like that better."

"So would I." Silvia's smile was shy. With a sigh she said, "That's something Rico and I have in common you know. I lost my father too. And my mother. I was eight when they were killed, so I remember them." She leaned her head on Sarah's shoulder. "My father was handsome, even more handsome than Uncle Andres. He was fun too, always laughing and teasing."

Silvia picked up a piece of straw and began to worry it with her fingers. "My mother was beautiful. She had velvet-black hair and big brown eyes that were fringed with the longest eyelashes in the world. Her skin was soft and she always smelled so good. Sometimes I lie in bed at night and I remember how she smelled." Her voice fell to a whisper. "I wish they hadn't died. I wish I could talk to them and . . ."

Sarah pulled the girl closer and kissed the top of her head.

"It wouldn't be so bad maybe," Silvia went on, "if I had a brother or sister. It's terrible being an only child." She looked up at Sarah. "Do you have brothers and sisters?"

Sarah shook her head. "I'm an only child too."

"Grandmother Teresa is wonderful. I worry a lot because I know she's not well and that . . . that scares me. Uncle Andres is nice and I know he loves me but he's so busy with the ranch that he doesn't have much time for me." She hesitated. "I'm sorry Rico was hurt, Sarah, but it's going to be nice having the two of you here for the summer. Will it be all right if I help you take care of him?"

"Of course it will. I'd—"

"Silvia?" Andres's voice broke in. "Silvia, are you in here?"

The girl looked at Sarah, bottom lip caught between her teeth. With a sigh she said, "Yes, Uncle Andres. I'm in here with Princesa."

He opened the stall door. "Your grandmother is worried about you. She . . ." He saw Sarah. One eyebrow rose as Sarah and Silvia stood up and brushed the straw off their jeans.

"Your grandmother's waiting up for you," he said to the girl.

"I'm sorry, Uncle Andres. Sarah and I were talking."

"Were you?" His voice hardened. "It's late, Silvia. Go along, please."

"Yes, Uncle Andres." She glanced at Sarah and said, "Shall we go?"

Sarah nodded, eager to escape. But before she'd taken two steps Andres said, "Just a moment, Sarah. Silvia, you go ahead. I want to talk to Mrs. Carlson."

Silvia glanced quickly at Sarah. "I'll see you in the morning?" she asked.

"Of course." Impulsively Sarah kissed Silvia's cheek. "Don't worry about Richard, he's going to be fine."

She waited until the girl went out and closed the stable door behind her before she turned to face Andres. "Please," she said, holding her hands in front of her as though defending herself. "It's been a long day,

Andres. I'm tired. I want to get back to Richard. Can't we put this off until tomorrow?''

"It's been put off for fifteen years, Sarah."

She looked at him, then away.

"I want to know about Richard." He took a deep breath. "He's Carlos's son, isn't he?"

"No!" Sarah steeled herself to meet his gaze. "I don't know what you're talking about, Andres."

"Don't you?" His voice was dangerous. "It was so obvious that I don't know why it took me until today to see it. Rico's just like Carlos. He has his features, his coloring, his build."

"You're out of your mind." Sarah backed away from him, trying not to panic. "His father was Peter Carlson. He was Portuguese. He—"

"With a name like Carlson?"

"I told you, the family changed it."

"From what?"

"I . . . I don't remember."

Andres took a menacing step toward her. "You don't remember because there never was a Peter Carlson. He was a figment of your imagination, an imaginary husband to cover the fact that Richard is illegitimate."

"No!" Sarah's hands tightened into fists as she faced him. "I was married to Peter Carlson. He was Portuguese. We were married in Miami on the—"

"You're lying." Andres grabbed her and shook her hard. "Damn you," he snarled. "Tell me the truth."

"Let me go!" Sarah struggled to free herself.

"Not until you tell me the truth." His eyes burned into hers. His fingers dug into her arms. "Damn you, Sarah, tell me the truth. Is Rico Carlos's son?"

She felt as though she were drowning in the black fury of his eyes. She tried to summon the strength to defy him and her body tensed, ready to fight.

"Tell me," he said again. "Or I swear I'll—"

"Andres, don't." Sarah took a deep breath and tried to get a rein on her emotions. "Can't we…can't we just leave it alone?"

He shook his head. "No, Sarah. I want the truth and I want it now. He is Carlos's son, isn't he?"

"Yes," Sarah said in a hollow voice. "He's Carlos's son." She thought for a moment her legs wouldn't support her and that if Andres let go of her she would surely fall.

His hands tightened so hard on her arms that she winced. "Why didn't you tell Carlos?" Andres demanded in a voice made raw by anger. "He had the right to know."

"The right?" Sarah stared at him. "What right? I didn't mean anything to Carlos. I was only a summer romance, a dumb little gringa that he'd set out to seduce."

"Don't play the innocent with me, Sarah. I was here that summer, I remember the way it was." Suddenly all of the fury that he'd held bottled up for so long spilled out; fury at the dead brother who had taken the young Sarah; and yes, fury at himself. He knew deep down in the dark places of his soul that he too had wanted Sarah fifteen years before.

Now in his anger he said, "I remember the way you flirted with him. You teased Carlos. You led him on and—"

"That's not fair. I didn't do that and if I did I didn't mean it."

"You didn't mean it?" Andres laughed. "Come on, Sarah, you may have been young but you knew what you were doing."

"No, I didn't!" She pulled out of his grasp and turning away from him leaned on the half door of the empty stall. "You don't understand," she said in a low voice. "I...I hadn't had that much experience with boys—with men." She closed her eyes, wondering how she could explain to Andres how it had been for her. He had a preconceived notion of what American girls were like. But she hadn't been like most girls; her parents hadn't been like most parents.

Mexico had been a wonderful escape for her. For the first time in her life she'd been free. It had been a heady feeling, especially when Carlos began to pay attention to her.

"It's hard to explain the way it was," Sarah said.

A muscle jumped in his face. "All right. So you and Carlos made love."

"Once," she said, meeting his gaze. "Only once."

Carlos had told the truth, Andres thought with a shock of pain. He remembered his brother's words: "She was a virgin, Andres."

His face was white, his voice strained when he said, "You should have told Carlos when you found out you were pregnant, Sarah."

"What good would it have done? Carlos was engaged to Maria Escobar—as you so bluntly told me the day before I left."

"Carlos would have helped you, Sarah. The family would have helped you."

"I didn't need their help."

"Your parents . . . ? How did they take it?"

"My mother opted for an abortion; my father suggested adoption." Her hands tightened on the half door. "I went to live with my aunt in Miami."

"I'm sorry." For the first time since he had found her here in the stable his voice softened. "It must have been a rough time for you."

"I survived." Sarah looked at him now and her face was cold. "I didn't want to come back. I never wanted to see Guadalajara again. But Richard's Spanish class was coming and I said he could go. A few days before they were to leave one of the chaperones got sick. They asked me to take her place because I spoke Spanish. I came back because of Richard. It was only going to be for three weeks."

"You've got to tell him."

"What?" Sarah looked at him blankly. "What do you mean?"

"Sarah, he's got to know who his real father was."

"No!" The cry tore from Sarah's throat. Her hands clutched her stomach as though she were in pain. "No!" she cried again.

"You have to. Richard has a right to know. He has the right to his heritage."

"He *has* a heritage."

"What? Grandparents who didn't want him to be born? An apartment in Miami?" Andres turned her around to face him. "El Camichín belongs to him, Sarah. And Richard belongs to it. Can't you see that? From the moment he set foot on the ranch he belonged. He loves it here. I don't think he even minds the wound because it's going to keep him here for a while."

"I won't tell him," Sarah shouted, out of control now. "I won't say, 'Oh, by the way, Richard, there's something I've been meaning to tell you for the last fifteen years. You see, dear, your father wasn't really Peter Carlson because there never was a Peter Carlson. I chose our last name so that you'd have something of your father's—Carlos, Carl's son. Wasn't that clever of me?'"

Tears were streaming down Sarah's face but she wasn't aware of them. "'Your real father was Carlos Navarro,' I'll say. 'I was his twenty-first birthday present.'"

"Stop it! Damn you, stop it!"

"'I'd been flirting, teasing him, dear, at least that's what your Uncle Andres says, so of course what happened was my fault even though I tried to...'" Sarah put her fist against her mouth to try to stop the words that would not be stopped. "I should have screamed," she whispered. "I should have but I didn't—"

Andres grabbed her. He shook her until her hair fell around her face, until she whimpered in pain from the hands that clasped her so tightly. She looked up at Andres, her eyes wide, her lips parted. Then she crumbled and would have fallen if he hadn't held her.

"I'm sorry." He pulled her roughly into his arms and held her, his hand against her tumbled hair.

The tears came again and not even knowing that she did, Sarah clung to him. She wept for all the lost years, for herself and for Richard. She wept for Carlos. She wept because she knew she could never have the only man she'd ever loved, this man who held her in his arms.

"It's all right, Sarah," Andres whispered against her hair.

But it wasn't all right. It never could be.

Andres kissed her temple, his lips warm against her skin. "Sarah," he sighed and tasted the salt tears on her parted lips. He wanted to take away the pain that her words had cost, he told himself. She felt so good in his arms, so soft, so warm.

The kiss deepened and Sarah was lost, a willing captive of the arms that held her and of the mouth that demanded a response. When he cupped her breasts she trembled against him and answered his kiss with a hunger as urgent as his.

Electric stabs of feeling shuddered through her. She whispered his name against his lips and heard him gasp with pleasure as the kiss deepened. Then, as suddenly as it had begun, it ended.

Andres thrust Sarah away from him. "No!" he said.

"What...?"

"No, I can't." He ran a distracted hand through his black hair. "You belonged to Carlos." His voice shook with emotion as his hands dropped to his sides. "I'm sorry, Sarah. This was my fault. I shouldn't have..." He turned away from her.

Sarah stood still as death as all of the humiliation, all of the shame she'd felt so long ago came rushing back. Then she straightened her shoulders. "Of course, Andres," she said stiffly. "I understand."

He looked at her now with a remote face and eyes that avoided hers. He seemed like a stranger. When they left the stable he tried to take Sarah's arm, but she stepped away from him.

From somewhere in the quiet distance a dog barked. It was a lonely sound, a cold and chilling sound—as cold as the space around her heart that only a short time ago had been warmed by love.

Chapter Nine

Sarah tried to sleep on the chaise in Richard's room that night. Twice she woke him to give him the antibiotic that Dr. Olsina had left. When he said, "My leg hurts, Mom," she gave him a painkiller.

In the darkness of the night she held Richard's hand, waiting until she was sure he would sleep before she went back to the chaise. She couldn't sleep. She thought of how Andres had thrust her away from him as though she were too soiled for him to touch and her face burned with shame. How could she face him again? And dear God, what was she going to do now that he knew about Richard?

Her son was the most important person in her life. He trusted her. How could she tell him that she'd lied to him about his father? How could she say, There never was a marriage? There never was a husband. You're illegitimate.

There in the darkness Sarah buried her face in her hands. Andres would force her to tell Richard the truth. If she didn't he would. He said Richard had to know about his heritage. Did that mean he wanted Richard to be a Navarro? That he wanted Richard to stay here on the ranch?

A chill seeped into Sarah's bones and she pulled her robe closer about her body. Did Andres want to take her son away from her?

It was early morning she went into the kitchen to make a cup of coffee. When she had made it she sank into a chair, cupping her hands around the cup to warm them. She didn't hear Andres until he opened the kitchen door. Her hands tightened around the cup as she stared at him.

"Good morning," he said. "How's Rico?"

"He had a lot of pain during the night. He's sleeping now."

"That's good. Dr. Olsina will be here soon." He looked at Sarah's cup. "Is there any more coffee?"

"Yes, I made a pot." She stood up. "I'd better get back to Richard."

"Aren't you going to finish your coffee?"

"No, I . . ."

"Sit down for a minute, Sarah. I'd like to talk to you."

"But I've got to get back to Richard."

"You said he was sleeping." Andres pulled out her chair. "Please sit down," he said.

She hadn't looked at Andres when he first came in, but now she did. She saw the dark shadows under his eyes and knew that he hadn't slept any better than she had. He went to the stove to pour himself a cup of coffee, then came back to the table, pulled out a chair, and sat down opposite her.

"I told you last night that Richard has to be told that he's a Navarro."

"Andres, please listen to me. I can't—"

"Let me finish." His face was set and uncompromising. "Richard is going to be fifteen, he's almost a man. He has the right to know who his father was and the right to decide what he wants to do with his life." He looked at Sarah over the cup of steaming coffee. "This is his land, Sarah, Navarro land. Richard belongs here."

"He's my son," she said. "He belongs in Miami with me."

"In Miami?" As though brushing away a fly Andres swept the idea aside. "There are several private schools in Guadalajara, he can start there in the fall. Then prep school and a good university, one that specializes in either agronomy or animal husbandry."

"You can't do this." Sarah stared at him. "I won't let you decide his life for him this way. Richard is my son. He—"

"He's a Navarro! And by God, Sarah, if you don't tell him I will!"

Sarah looked into the uncompromising black eyes. All of the resentment she'd felt fifteen years ago came rushing back. He'd hated her then, and he hated her now.

"My mother and Silvia have to be told too," he said.

Sarah put her head down on the table, unable to believe this was happening. At last she raised her face and looking at Andres said, "Very well, I'll tell Richard. But not now, Andres. Not when he's been hurt."

He nodded. "But don't wait too long, Sarah. Richard's waited too many years as it is to know that Carlos was his father. He—"

A startled cry stopped his words. He looked up and saw his mother, as pale as death, swaying in the doorway.

"Dear God," he heard Sarah whisper. Then he was on his feet, catching his mother before she slumped unconscious to the floor.

Dr. Olsina arrived just as Andres ran into the *sala*, his mother in his arms.

"Good heavens!" Olsina cried. "What happened?"

"Mother's had a shock, she fainted." Andres laid her down on the sofa.

"Let me see her." The doctor bent over Teresa Navarro. He checked her pulse, frowned, then quickly opening his bag soaked a piece of cotton in alcohol and held it under her nose.

"Teresa," he said. "Teresa, can you hear me?"

"*Sí*, I . . ." She saw Sarah standing next to Andres and half rising from the sofa said, "Sarah, *ay Dios*, Sarah, is it true?"

"Shh." Gently Dr. Olsina eased her back against the cushions. "Don't alarm yourself, Teresa. I want you to rest while I take a look at you."

"But—"

"No, don't talk now. I want to listen to your heart."

When he finished his examination he said, "Andres is going to take you to your room. I'll give you something to quiet you down a bit. You'll feel better after you've rested." He motioned to Andres. "Can you carry her or shall I get you some help?"

"Of course I can carry her." Andres bent down and lifted his mother into his arms. "No argument, Mother," he said. He shot a look at Sarah as he shouldered past her.

"Will she be all right?" Sarah asked before the doctor turned to hurry after Andres.

"I'm not sure yet. Her heart's doing a Mexican Hat Dance. What happened? Did something upset her?"

Sarah twisted her hands. "Yes, I'm . . . I'm afraid so."

"I'd suggest that she not have any further upsets, Señora Carlson. Her heart won't take it. Having your boy hurt yesterday was a bad jolt. She seems to be very fond of him."

"Yes," Sarah managed to say. "Yes, she's fond of him."

"I'll take care of her, then I'll have a look at Richard. How is he this morning?"

"He had a restless night. I gave him the antibiotics you left."

"That's fine. I'm sure there's nothing to worry about as long as he doesn't get an infection. Now if you'll excuse me I'll look in on Señora Navarro."

Sarah tried to put everything out of her mind as she hurried down the corridor to Richard's room. But her face was taut with worry. What if something happened to Teresa Navarro? she thought. Teresa had heard Andres, she knew that Richard was Carlos's son. How would it affect her? Oh God, Sarah prayed, don't let anything happen to her.

She hesitated for a moment outside Richard's door, then trying to force a smile, opened it. "Hi, darling," she said when she saw that he was awake. "How are you doing?"

"Pretty good, Mom."

"How's the leg?"

"Okay." He grimaced. "It hurts, Mom. It hurts like hell."

She let the word go by. "I'll give you something for the pain just as soon as Dr. Olsina has seen you." She helped him sit up, then fluffed his pillows. His face was pale and there were shadows under his eyes. "I'm sorry I messed up, Mom. What are you going to do about your job?"

"I'll phone Miami later on and ask for a six-week leave. I'm sure it will be all right."

"What about the chaperoning? Will Miss Carney be mad?"

"I don't think so, Richard. I'll phone her too. As soon as you're feeling a little better I'll go into Guadalajara and talk to her. I—"

She stopped when there was a knock. When she said, "Come in," the doctor opened the door.

"How's my young matador this morning?" he asked with a smile. "I hear you're a pretty good man with the *muleta*."

"Really? Where did you hear that?"

"Andres told me that you did remarkably well for your first time in a ring. He said you stood your ground and that you made several decent passes before you were caught. Now then, let's have a look at that leg." He turned to Sarah. "This going to bother you or would you rather stay?"

"I'll stay." Sarah moved to the head of the bed so that she could stand close to Richard.

Olsina unwrapped the wound. It looked red and swollen but the doctor said, "Uh huh, hmm, yes, it's coming along." He pressed the flesh around it gently and when Richard flinched Olsina said, "Pains, doesn't it? Don't worry, another day or two and the pain will lessen."

After he'd put a fresh bandage on, he gave Richard another antibiotic. "Feel like breakfast?" he asked.

"Sure."

"That's a good sign. But after you've eaten I want you to take a nap. I'll be back tomorrow." To Sarah he said, "If you need anything in the meantime just call. Andres has my number. I'll look in again on Teresa before I go."

"Is something wrong with Grandmother Teresa?" Richard asked when the doctor had left his room. "What is it? What's the matter with her?"

"She just didn't feel very well, darling. But she'll be all right. Now what would you like for breakfast?"

One of the maids fixed Richard's breakfast and Sarah sat with him while he ate. She had just picked up his tray to take it to the kitchen when Silvia peeked in the door.

"Would it be all right if I said hello to Richard?" the girl said. "I just saw Dr. Olsina going into Grandmother's room. Is she sick, Sarah?"

Sarah put her arm around Silvia. "She's going to be all right," she said, "and so is our brave matador."

Silvia came hesitantly into the room. "How are you, Rico?" she whispered.

"The doc says I'm going to be okay but that it's really a terrible *cornada*." He looked at Sarah and said, "That's a horn wound, Mom."

"It's my fault." Silvia nibbled her bottom lip. "I teased you into going in the ring."

"Your fault?" Richard gave an ungentlemanly snort. "I'd known since all that business started in the morning that I'd get in the ring before the day was over. So don't be a dope, okay?"

"Look," Sarah said. "You two visit for a little while." She kissed Richard's forehead and to Silvia said, "You keep an eye on him for me."

She went out into the corridor just as Andres emerged from his mother's room. He stood for a moment, looking at Sarah before he started toward her.

"Mother wants to see you," he said.

"How is she? Did you...did she say anything about Richard?"

Andres shook his head. "I told her you'd talk to her. She's waiting for you."

"I see." There was no escape. Doña Teresa had overheard their conversation. This had to be faced.

"My mother's not well," Andres said. "If you say anything to upset her..." His voice was as hard as the hand that grasped her arm.

"She's already upset, Andres. All I can do now is tell her the truth about Richard."

"See that you do." Their gazes locked and held. It was Andres who looked away first. "I'll be out in the patio," he said. "I'd like to see you after you've talked to Mother."

Sarah nodded, and without a backward glance went down the corridor to Teresa Navarro's room.

The older woman's face was pale. Her dark eyes looked too large for her face.

"Tell me," she whispered from her bed. "Is that dear boy really my grandson?"

Sarah sat on the side of the bed and took Teresa's hand. "Yes," she said. "Richard is Carlos's son."

"I think I always knew, Sarah. I felt something the first time I saw Rico." Her hand tightened on Sarah's. "Can you tell me about it, Sarah?"

So Sarah told her, as gently as she could, what had happened between her and Carlos that summer long ago. "We were young," she said. "We were attracted to each other." She smiled gently at Teresa. "Carlos was so handsome. I loved his laughter and his gaiety."

"Did you know you were pregnant when you were here, Sarah? Is that why you went home?"

"No, Doña Teresa, I didn't know until after I'd returned to Chicago."

"But why didn't you let us know? We would have helped you. Carlos would have married you."

Sarah shook her head. "His life had been planned, Doña Teresa. I knew there'd never be room enough in it for me."

"You knew about the engagement to Maria?"

"Andres told me."

"But Carlos had an obligation to you. You shouldn't have had to face your pregnancy alone." She reached up and touched Sarah's face. "It must have been a difficult time for you, Sarah." Her brows raised in question. "But you did marry? Later I mean?"

"No, Doña Teresa, I never married. I . . . I invented a husband. I told Richard that his father had died before he was born."

For a moment Teresa Navarro didn't speak. She looked at Sarah, her dark eyes filled with compassion. "Now you are wondering whether or not to tell Rico the truth about his father, aren't you?"

"Andres says that if I don't he will."

"He will not!" Teresa pulled herself to an upright position. "Send him to me. I won't allow—"

"Shh." Sarah eased Teresa back against the pillows. "You're not to worry about this."

"It was Andres who discovered the truth, wasn't it?"

"When he saw Richard in the bullring. He looked at Richard and suddenly he knew." For the first time since she had come into the room a look of anguish crossed Sarah's face. "I know I have to tell Richard," she said. "But oh, Doña Teresa, it's going to be hard. It's going to be so hard."

"I know, child. But it will be all right. This is Richard's home, Sarah. This is where he belongs. It's his land, his and Andres's and Silvia's." Her hand tightened on Sarah's. "With all my heart I thank you for giving me a grandson," she said.

Andres was waiting for Sarah when she went out to the patio. Without waiting for him to speak, or acknowledging his presence, Sarah went to the fountain. She stared down at the gently bubbling water, then sat down and waited for Andres to speak.

"You talked to Mother?" he asked.

"Yes. She's resting. She didn't take it like I expected her to."

"And how did you expect her to take it?"

"I was afraid she might think Richard and I were interlopers, that I'd come here deliberately to try...to try to make some claim on the land. But she was pleased. I think..." Sarah swallowed hard. "I think she feels that she's gotten a small part of Carlos back."

"Did you love him?"

"What?"

"Dammit, I asked you if you'd loved Carlos."

Sarah stared up at Andres, almost too startled for a moment to speak. His eyes bored into hers, demanding an answer.

"No," she said at last. "I didn't love him. I was too young. I didn't know what it meant to love somebody. I liked Carlos. I..." She took a deep breath. "No, Andres, I wasn't in love with him."

She looks so tired, Andres thought. So defeated. For a moment he wanted to put his arms around her, but he couldn't.

The night before in the stable when he had kissed her, he'd known that she wanted him as much as he wanted her. Her lips had parted to receive his kiss. He'd felt the soft yielding of her body. He'd known that if he had carried her into the empty stall and laid her on the sweet-smelling hay she would have given herself to him.

But he hadn't taken her because he'd thought of Carlos. And suddenly he knew he couldn't touch

Sarah because the thought of her having been with Carlos, of bearing Carlos's child, had been more than he could stand. He didn't want her; he didn't want to touch her.

It's too late for us, he thought bitterly. I had the only chance I was ever going to have fifteen years ago. It's too late now. As soon as Richard is well she'll go back to her own country.

But I will have her son, Andres thought. I will have Sarah's son.

Chapter Ten

That afternoon Sarah phoned Rachel Carney.

"I'm so sorry," Rachel said when Sarah told her about Richard's accident. "The poor kid. How's he doing?"

"He's having a lot of discomfort, Rachel, but he loves the idea that he has to stay here for a month and a half."

"What about you? Good Lord, Sarah, what about your job?"

"I phoned my boss an hour ago. He was upset but he understands." Sarah barely suppressed a sigh. "How are the kids doing?"

"Okay. They love school. My only problem so far has been trying to keep Harvey Hartman away from

Marilee. Even though the girls are on one floor and the boys are on another, it's hard to keep Harvey where he belongs. The kid's got a nonstop libido."

"I'm sorry I've let you down, Rachel."

"It can't be helped. I know you want to be with Richard."

"For a couple more days at least. As soon as I know he's going to be all right I'll come to Guadalajara."

"We're going to the university on Thursday, Sarah, then out to Tlaquepaque. It would be a big help if you could manage that."

"Count on me, Rachel. Silvia and I will both be there."

On Thursday morning Silvia said, "I don't think we should both leave Rico, Sarah. I'll be glad to stay home with him."

"He'll be fine," Sarah assured her. "Your grandmother's better. She can look in on him and so can the maids."

Teresa, once she'd gotten over the initial shock of learning that Richard was Carlos's son, had improved rapidly.

"I feel as though the clock has been turned back," she told Sarah. "It's almost as though I have my son back again. You can't imagine how that makes me feel, Sarah. I've been given a new lease on life and I have you to thank for it."

They discussed the problem of telling Richard the truth about his father. Teresa agreed that nothing be

said until he had recovered from the goring, and that
when he was told he would hear it from Sarah.

Sarah had seen little of Andres since the morning his
mother had been taken ill, and even though she worried about Richard, it was a relief to be away from the
ranch on Thursday. Silvia was bright, cheerful and fun
to be with. Since the night in the barn they'd grown
closer. Silvia confided her hopes and her dreams to
Sarah and for the first time in Sarah's life she sensed
what it might be like to have a daughter.

They went into Guadalajara on Friday, too, and returned to the ranch in time for dinner. As she had since
Richard's injury, Sarah ate her dinner with him in his
room. "This is the last weekend Miss Carney and the
students will be here," she told him. "They've planned
an outing at Lake Chapala and they need an extra
chaperone. If you don't mind, I really think I should
go."

"Sure, Mom. It's okay." But he looked dejected. "I
really wanted to see Lake Chapala."

"We'll go as soon as you're well." Sarah almost
said, "Before we go home," but she wasn't sure
Richard would be going home. Then, trying to put the
thought to the back of her mind she sat beside him on
the bed. "I'm sorry you're missing out on things,
honey. I know this trip hasn't turned out the way you
planned."

"It's turned out better than I planned, Mom. I miss
the kids, but I'd a thousand times rather be here at the
ranch, even if I am in bed. It's not like I'm a stranger

here. Grandmother Teresa comes in every morning
after you leave. She's been telling me all about the
Navarros and it's interesting. Did you know the first
Navarro came to Mexico with Cortés in 1519? He
married an Aztec princess and never went back to
Spain. Can you imagine a family history like that?''

It's part of your history too, Sarah wanted to tell
him, because you're a Navarro, Richard, and soon I'll
have to tell you that you are. But she said nothing, just
ruffled his hair and promised to call him on Saturday
night.

She and Silvia shared a room at the hotel on the
shore of the lake. "Wouldn't you rather be with a girl
your own age?" Sarah asked her.

"No, I want to be with you so we can talk. It's all
right, isn't it? I mean if you'd rather be alone . . .''

"Of course I wouldn't rather be alone." Sarah
hugged her. "I love having you for a roommate."

They spent the day at the beach, and that afternoon
when one of the boys wanted to teach Silvia to water-
ski, Sarah thought of another afternoon and another
boy. For a moment the memory of that day long ago
overwhelmed her.

After dinner that evening she and Silvia telephoned
Richard.

"Everything's okay," he said. "We're going to have
a cookout on the patio tomorrow if Andres isn't too
busy. He's hardly been here at all for meals but he's
pretty sure he'll make it tomorrow. There's been some
kind of a problem with the bulls. The other night one

of them broke out of the pasture and it took Andres and a couple of the workmen all night to get it corralled. He hasn't even come home the last few nights. He's got a cabin near the bullring and he's been staying there. He's promised to be here for the cookout though, so he can carry me out to the patio. You sure you and Silvia won't get back in time so you can be here, too?"

"I'm afraid not, Richard. The bus won't pick us up until six. With all the heavy Sunday traffic we probably won't get back to Guadalajara until eight or so. We should be able to make it to the ranch by nine."

It was in fact almost ten-thirty before Sarah and Silvia returned to El Camichín. The house was quiet, and except for a light in the *sala* the rest of the house was dark. Sarah walked Silvia to her room, kissed her good-night, then went down the hall to Richard's room. He was awake, watching television in the dark. They talked for a while and when Sarah was sure he was all right she kissed him and went to her own room.

After she had undressed and taken a shower she moved restlessly around her room. She picked up a book, then put it down. For the past few days she'd been too busy to think about Andres and having to tell Richard the truth about his father. Now that she was back at El Camichín all of the worry she'd had since the day of Richard's goring came rushing back. She paced up and down, knowing she wouldn't be able to sleep unless she walked some of her tension away.

Not bothering with underwear or shoes, Sarah pulled on a pair of shorts and a T-shirt and slipped out through the French doors. She stood for a moment breathing in the scent of jasmine, then crossed the patio and by the light of a half moon found the path leading down to the pastures.

As Sarah walked she felt herself relax. The air was soft, the ground felt good beneath her bare feet. When she came to a stone wall she leaned against it and breathed in the good smell of loam and clover. She loved this land almost as much as Richard did. For the first time since Andres had learned that Richard was Carlos's son, she admitted to herself Andres was right—Richard had to be told the truth. He was a Navarro. He had the blood of the Spaniard and of the Aztec running through his veins. He was a part of this country.

Near her, somewhere in the darkness, Sarah heard a movement.

"Who is it? Who's there?" she asked as a chill of fear ran through her body. She tried to see but a cloud had covered the moon.

Sarah peered through the darkness. Suddenly she sensed a faint animal odor, and as the cloud moved away from the moon she saw the bull. She saw the flick of his tail, the slight lowering of his head, and the glimmer of moonlight on the sharp white horns.

She couldn't move. She was rooted to the spot, held by a terror unlike anything she'd ever known, unaware that perspiration ran down her body in salty rivulets.

He can hear my heart, Sarah thought. Then she didn't think at all.

Andres heard Sarah come in. He watched from the window of his bedroom as she and Silvia crossed the patio to the *sala*. He listened to their footsteps, to the closing of Sarah's door. He'd hardly seen her since the day his mother had overheard them talking in the kitchen. When he had seen her it was only to say, *"Buenos días"* or *"buenas tardes."* He was aware that she looked pale and drawn, and told himself that it was because she was worried about Richard. But he knew that wasn't all of it, for when she looked at him there was fear in her golden eyes. He knew she was waiting, like a small bird waited for the giant tom to pounce, for him to say, "Today, Sarah. Tell Richard today."

It would be hard for Sarah, he knew that. But Richard had to be told because he had the right to choose the kind of life he would lead.

It had been a long day and Andres was tired. He started to turn away from the window when he saw Sarah emerge from the French doors leading to her room. He caught the glint of moonlight on her fair hair and saw her slender body silhouetted by the patio light. He felt his breath catch in his throat and knew a sudden hot rush of desire, a desire so strong it took every bit of his willpower not to rush out and carry her back to his room.

Would Sarah have come willingly? He remembered how it had been that night in the stable. She would fight me because I've hurt her, Andres thought. But in the end her lips would soften under mine, her body would yield.

His hand was already on the doorknob when he stopped, because the thought of Carlos intruded on his desire for Sarah. She'd belonged to his brother; she could never belong to him. He went back to the window and watched as she disappeared down the path, into the darkness.

Andres sat on the edge of the bed and took off his boots. He pulled his shirt out of his jeans and had just started to unbutton it. Sarah had headed in the direction of the pastures. He remembered the bull that had gotten loose, a maverick that refused to be a part of the herd. It had taken him, José, Manolo and Paco to get the beast back into the corral when daylight came. Poor Manolo had suffered a slash on his arm that had required twelve stitches and a tetanus shot. Andres didn't like the idea of Sarah wandering off by herself at night. The chances were a hundred to one that the bull would escape again, but what if it did?

Without conscious thought Andres burst through the doors leading to the patio, down the path that Sarah had taken.

Nothing's going to happen to her, he told himself. But his heart beat hard against his ribs and his mouth was dry. He ran faster, spurred on by his fear.

In the light of the moon he saw Sarah, standing as still as death. Not ten feet from her stood the renegade bull, head lowered, ready to charge.

"Sarah," Andres said softly as he started toward her, forcing himself to move slowly. "Easy," he cautioned her. "Don't move, don't—"

It was too late. The bull charged. Andres heard the startled gasp of a shortened scream, then the impact of the animal's body against Sarah's before she fell.

"Ya, toro!" Andres yelled the call at the top of his voice, ripping the shirt off his back waving it toward the bull as he ran. "Cover your head!" he screamed at Sarah. "Roll away!"

The bull butted against her as she rolled herself into a ball. She smelled the beast's saliva and her own terrible fear. Andres shouted another bloodcurdling cry. The bull wheeled and charged him.

"Over the wall!" Andres cried. "Get over the wall!"

Sarah tried to get up. On her hands and knees she watched the bull charge. Andres held the shirt to the side as he would a cape. The animal passed, barely missing his body.

"Dammit, get over the wall!"

Sarah staggered to her feet, backing to the wall, watching Andres and the bull. The stone felt cold against her hands as she turned and half fell, half threw herself up over the top onto the other side. Then she climbed to her feet to watch the man and the beast who were silhouetted in the moonlight. Teresa had called it a tragic ballet, but there was no orchestration here in this field. No curtain would fall when it was over, for there would be no one to take a bow.

Suddenly Sarah yanked her T-shirt over her head, and as Andres had done, she began to wave it, half hanging over the wall, screaming a witch's cry in her terrible fear.

The bull turned away and raced for the wall as Sarah fell back. Then Andres vaulted over and landed beside her.

"Are you all right?" he gasped. "Did the horns catch you anywhere? Are you hurt?"

"I . . . I don't think so."

Andres picked her up, and holding her close to his body so that he wouldn't jar her, began to run toward the bullring. He reached the cabin, opened the door and carried Sarah inside.

When he had laid her on the sofa he turned on a light. "Let me take a look at you," he said. It was then Sarah realized she was bare from the waist up. But it didn't seem to matter, Andres's interest in her was strictly clinical. He ran his hands up and down her arms. Carefully he pressed her ribs. "Any pain here?" he asked.

Sarah shook her head. "He hit me in the stomach," she said.

Andres undid the button of her shorts and pulled them partway down before she could protest. He pressed his fingers against her flesh. "That hurt?"

"It's just sore."

Andres looked relieved. "You took a hard blow but I don't think it's anything serious."

"What about the bull? Shouldn't you do something about him?"

"There isn't anything I can do tonight. The boys will round him up tomorrow." He pulled a quilted throw off the back of the sofa and handed it to Sarah. "What in hell were you doing wandering around this time of night?"

"I just wanted some air. I'd been surrounded by dozens of noisy kids all day. I guess I . . . wanted to be alone." She looked at him curiously. "How did you know where I was?"

"I saw you from my window. A bull had broken loose a couple of days ago. I knew the chances were a thousand to one that it would ever happen again but I didn't want to take that chance."

Sarah shivered. "Thank God you didn't."

"Would you like a drink? We both need one." Andres went to a wall cabinet, opened it and took out a bottle of brandy. When he had poured a small amount in two glasses he brought one to Sarah. "Drink this while I run a hot tub for you. If you don't try to soak the soreness out right away you won't be able to move tomorrow."

Sarah pulled the quilted wrap around her. "If you'll loan me a shirt I'll go back to the house."

"With the bull wandering around out in the darkness?" Andres shook his head. "You'll be better off here with me, Sarah. At least I don't have horns."

Sarah looked at him. She wasn't so sure.

Five minutes later she lowered herself into a steaming tub of hot water. Her stomach hurt and she'd begun to shiver with reaction. But the hot water soothed her. She put her head back against the tub and closed her eyes, remembering that terrible moment when the bull had charged, and tried not to think what would have happened if Andres hadn't arrived on the scene.

When she stepped out of the tub she took a white terry cloth robe off the hook behind the door, put it on and belted it around her.

"Another drink?" Andres asked when Sarah came out of the bathroom.

"No thanks."

"You can have the bedroom." He indicated an open door behind him. "I'll sleep on the sofa."

"Thank you, Andres. Thank you for coming to my rescue."

"You're welcome." He didn't look at her. "I put a pair of pajamas out on the bed. I'll probably be up before you are in the morning. Don't leave until you hear from me or one of the men."

"All right." Sarah looked at him and he looked away. When she went into the bedroom she put on his pajamas. She lay in his bed, there in the darkness, trying not to think of the bull, willing herself not to think of Andres—and at last she slept.

In her dream she saw Richard coming toward her. She called to him. He didn't hear her. She waved. He didn't see her. "The bull!" she screamed, but no sound came from her throat. She tried to run, but something held her back. She could smell the bull, see the saliva drip from his mouth as he lowered his head to charge.

"Run, Richard!" she screamed.

He looked toward her and began to move. One slow step, then two. The bull raced toward him and she screamed—and screamed and screamed...

"Sarah!" Someone gripped her shoulder. "Sarah, wake up!"

"It's Richard, he..." She opened her eyes. By the light from the other room she saw Andres beside her. "It was Richard," she whispered. "He couldn't run. He..." She shuddered. "I thought...I thought he—"

"It was only a dream." Andres put his arm around her.

Sarah clung to him, needing the assurance of his arms holding her close. "I couldn't stand it if something happened to Richard," she said as she clutched Andres's shoulders. "I was so frightened tonight, Andres. I could smell the bull. I'll never be able to forget that smell or the sound he made just before he charged. It was a low throaty growl. I knew he was going to charge but I couldn't move."

"You're safe, Sarah," Andres murmured against her hair. "I won't let anything happen to you." He could feel her heart beating violently against his chest. Before he knew what he was going to do he lay down beside her so he could hold her close and tell her that she was safe. He was with her and she didn't need to be afraid. First he whispered the words against her lips, then he kissed her.

It felt so good to be there in the warm comfort of Andres's arms. When he kissed her she thought, I'll only stay like this for a moment. But the kiss deepened and still Sarah didn't move away. Her hands crept up around the back of his neck. She touched the silky hairs there, then threaded her fingers through the thickness of his hair.

Andres pressed her close so that the whole long male length of him was against her. Sarah broke away from his kiss. "Andres," she whispered. "Andres, I—"

He took her mouth again. His lips were fierce, hard and uncompromising against hers as he urged her closer. With frantic fingers he tore at the buttons of the pajama top, ripping them away in his need to touch her. He crushed Sarah against him. She felt the thick mat of chest hair against her bare breasts as he kissed her again.

Sarah was lost now, lost in the feel of his body against hers, in the mouth that possessed hers, in the arms that held her captive.

When Andres held her away from him Sarah looked at him, her lips parted, her eyes dazed by desire.

Without speaking he laid her back against the pillows and bent to kiss her breasts.

Sarah's fingers tightened on his shoulders. I can't let him do this, she thought. Not after what he's done. I can't... She tried to pull away but Andres held her. His tongue flicked against her nipple and she cried out.

"Let me love you," he said against her skin. "Let me love you, Sarah."

She'd never known such a sweet torture as he kissed first one breast, then the other until she shook with need. Her hands roamed over his shoulders and down his arms, marveling in the feel, the texture of his skin. His hand slipped into the bottom of her pajamas, cupping her and Sarah turned her face into his shoulder, feeling shivers of pleasure running up and down her body. He let her go to pull the pajama bottoms down over her hips—then his own.

For a moment Andres held her close to him, one hand against the nape of her neck, the other on the small of her back. He didn't speak, not even to say her name, simply holding her while she felt his body tremble with need. He rolled her onto her back and knelt over her. His cave-black eyes were hooded with desire as he stared down at her. With a gasp of need he merged his body to hers.

Sarah cried out. Her muscles tightened as she remembered that other time. She tried to escape but Andres held her, his hands clasping her shoulders as he covered her, moving against her with an urgency that frightened her—until her own body filled with the same wonderful urgency. Sarah tightened her arms around him. Her mouth sought his. "Andres!" she cried softly, half in pleasure, half in fear. "Andres!"

"Little love," he said against her lips. "My sweet Sarah."

Sensation followed sensation as he carried Sarah up and up on a sweet tide of passion that was past bearing. She heard him cry her name and she was shattered like the bright and brilliant star colors of a kaleidoscope, whirling round and round in an endless frenzy of unparalleled joy.

They didn't speak. Sarah lay with her head on Andres's shoulder, feeling the frantic beat of his heart. His fingers spread through the softness of her hair, while the other caressed the silken length of her.

Sarah wanted him to say something to her. She wanted an assurance that he cared about her, that this had meant as much to him as it had to her. But Andres didn't speak; he just lay there beside her until she slept.

Later, Sarah didn't know when, she felt his hands on her breasts. She murmured sleepily against him, not opening her eyes as she moved into the warmth of his embrace. He didn't kiss her. He touched her breasts and his hands moved up and down her body until she whispered his name against his throat. Then quickly, fiercely, he took her, there in the stillness of the night.

It wasn't like the other time. It was as wild and angry as a storm. Andres's mouth was hard and demanding against hers and his hands tightened until her mouth softened and trembled under his. He ravaged her mouth as he ravaged her body and she cried out in both fear and passion as he took her higher and higher to a crest of feeling she'd never dreamed possible.

In her final moment of ecstasy, Sarah cried his name. He took her cry into his mouth as his body moved relentlessly against hers, taking and taking until she had nothing left to give before he gasped his own cry of release.

Andres brought her a cup of coffee in the morning. She yelped in pain when she tried to sit up and he saw that she had already started to turn black-and-blue from where she'd been hit by the bull.

"I'm going to round up the men." His voice was cool and matter-of-fact. "Go back to sleep. I'll send word up to the house about what happened and where you are. We'd better have Olsina look at you later."

Sarah nodded. She looked up at him, waiting for a word, a look of acknowledgment, a recognition of what had passed between them. She wanted him to touch her, wanted him to say her name.

All he said was, "Don't leave until someone tells you it's safe." Then he turned on his heel and without a backward look went out and left her alone.

Chapter Eleven

Andres had wanted to touch her, to take her in his arms and tell her that nothing mattered except what had passed between them. He knew that he had been rough with her that last time because he'd wanted to punish her for responding to him, as he'd wanted to punish himself for wanting her.

Andres had made love to a lot of other women in his life, experienced women skilled in the art of love. Sarah hadn't been skilled; she'd been awkward and unsure of herself. Yet he had found that inexperience more exciting than anything he'd ever known before. He thought of all the things he would teach her and knew that she would be a willing pupil. Last night she had answered his passion with a shyness and vulnerability that had touched him to the depths of his being. Her body had yielded to his, responded to his, and when she gave that first sharp cry of amazed joy he'd felt his whole body tremble with pleasure.

Sarah. How incredibly lovely she was. He remembered how her amber eyes had drifted slowly shut when he kissed her breasts. When finally she went to sleep he'd curled a lock of her golden hair around his finger and kissed her temple. Silently he'd told her all the things he'd never be able to speak.

Making love with you is unlike anything I've ever known before, he wanted to say. I didn't mean it to happen, Sarah, but I couldn't help myself. You were so warm in my arms, still lost in the nightmare of what had almost happened out there in the field. I felt your breasts against my chest, Sarah, your lips so close to mine, and I wanted you more than I've ever wanted anything in my life.

But I can't have you, Sarah, because a part of me will never forgive you for having belonged to Carlos first. I know you were young; I even know it wasn't your fault. But I can't forget it.

It was almost noon before Andres and his men rounded up the bull and herded the animal back to the enclosed pasture. Instead of going back to the cabin to tell Sarah it was safe to leave, he sent Paco. He didn't want to see her alone, there in the seclusion of his cabin, because he knew what would happen if he did.

For the next few days Andres stayed away from Sarah except at dinnertime when his mother and Silvia were present. The blow she had taken from the bull was more severe than he'd thought. Dr. Olsina had ordered Sarah to bed and he'd given her something to relieve the soreness and the pain. On the third day after the incident she'd come to the dinner table, walking carefully.

She looked at Andres, then away. When Doña Teresa murmured in sympathy Sarah smiled. "Richard says we're both veterans of the bullring now. I used to think big cities were dangerous. But I think I'd rather be mugged than attacked by a bull."

"I've never been anywhere in the United States except Texas," Silvia said. "I'd love to see Miami some day."

"Then you'll visit us. Richard and I..." Sarah glanced across the table at Andres and wet her lips. "We'd love to have you," she finished.

"Maybe I could go at Christmastime." Silvia turned to her grandmother. "Could I? I know you want me to spend Christmas Day here but maybe I could leave the day after."

The older woman looked at Sarah, then away. "We'll see," she said. "We'll talk it over with your Uncle Andres."

Silvia made a face. "But he's never here. Now that you've got that bull corralled, *Tío*, I hope you'll spend more time with us." She took a bite of her sweet potato. "I can't believe that Sarah almost got killed, that she would have if you hadn't rescued her. It's so romantic." She sighed and smiled at Sarah. "Uncle Andres rescuing you that way, having to stay in his cabin all night with the bull pawing and snorting at the door."

"Silvia!" Doña Teresa admonished. "Really!"

"The bull wasn't pawing at the door," Andres said dryly. "But he was out there somewhere so it wasn't safe to leave."

"Of course it wasn't." But for the first time since the incident Teresa looked questioningly at Sarah, then at her son. "It seems you're spending more and more time at the cabin, Andres. I don't understand it; you have a perfectly good room right here."

"I know, *madre*, but I've had a lot of things to attend to lately. I haven't wanted to come in late and disturb the rest of you."

"You wouldn't disturb us. I'd feel less disturbed knowing you were here."

Sarah kept her gaze on her plate, afraid to meet his eyes, afraid of what she would see there. Like the rest of the family, she'd seen little of Andres these past few days. It was obvious he stayed away from the house because of her. How he must resent me, she thought painfully. How he must hate having made love to me.

Each night after Sarah kissed Richard good-night she went to her room, but she slept little. All she could think about was Andres and how it had been with him.

A week after her accident with the bull Sarah went to him. When the house was dark and quiet she dressed in jeans and a sweater and slipped through the French doors, out across the patio to the path that led past the bullring. She hesitated when she reached the cabin, stopped for a moment, then with a deep breath went up the steps to the door. When she knocked she heard Andres say, "Yes? Who is it?"

She couldn't answer because her throat was so dry she couldn't speak. He opened the door, looked at her, then stepped aside. "Come in," he said.

"Andres..." Sarah wet her lips. "Andres, I came because I—"

"I know why you came." He took her hand and led her into the bedroom. There was a fire in the rough stone fireplace and he led her to it. "You're shaking." His face showed no emotion. "Are you cold?"

"No, I—"

Andres silenced her with a kiss so violent that she felt her legs weaken as her body swayed against him. When the kiss ended he held her away from him and without a word began to unfasten the buttons of her sweater. When he'd thrown it over a chair he turned her toward the fire so that he could look at her.

Her skin, in the light of the fire, was the color of a sun-kissed peach. Her eyes were smoky topaz. Andres ran his hands down her arms, then up to her shoulders and her breasts. He watched her lips part, her eyes widen.

"This is why you came," he said.

"No." Sarah quivered under his touch. "I wanted to talk to you."

"Liar." He pulled her back into his arms. Then he picked her up and carried her to the bed, his hunger for her so intense it was all he could do to hold himself back. Sarah was here, she had come to him. His arms tightened around her, his mouth covered hers.

I love him, Sarah thought. Oh, I do love him. He touched her breasts and she sighed with pleasure. He kissed her and her lips parted to receive his tongue. He trailed a line of fire down to her throat and she moaned with pleasure.

God, how he adored the taste of her skin, the scent of her body, the way she tensed and sighed when he touched her. The way she whispered his name when he kissed her breasts. Andres lowered his body on hers as a flame of feeling engulfed him. He grasped her hips, brought her body to his and slowly began to move against her.

Because Sarah couldn't say, "I love you, I've always loved you," she tried with her body to show him how she felt. She answered his fierceness with gentleness, his urgently possessive kiss with the sweetness of surrender. She offered her body, holding nothing back, her need as great as his as together they climbed the heights then tumbled in one last final rapturous embrace.

Andres didn't move from her. She could feel his breath against her lips, the racing of his heart. But she didn't speak. At last he left her and she waited, as she had before, for one word of kindness, one word of love.

Andres sat up. He ran a hand through his dark hair. He looked at Sarah and said, "That's why you came, isn't it?"

She turned away, unable to stop her tears of shame. She felt his hand on her hip. "Look at me," he said. When she didn't answer he brought her around to face him.

With an edge of the sheet he wiped her tears away. "I'm sorry if I hurt you. This—whatever it is between us—can't go on. We can never..." He turned away from her. "Nothing can come of this, Sarah. I want you to know that."

"Because of Carlos," she said in a flat voice. "Because of what happened fifteen years ago."

Andres nodded. "I can't forget it, Sarah. I wish I could. I want you. I look at you and I touch you, I make love to you and it's wonderful."

She saw the sadness in his dark eyes and bracing herself for what was to come said, "But?"

"I'm an anachronism, Sarah, an old-fashioned man who believes in old-fashioned virtues. I can't help it. Every time I make love to you I hate myself because I think of you with my brother."

Sarah stared up at him. Then she closed her eyes and turned away once more. When she heard him go into the other room she got up and dressed. When she was ready she went into the living room. Andres sat on the arm of the sofa, a snifter of brandy in his hand.

"Can I get you a drink?" His eyes didn't meet hers.

"No, thank you." Sarah waited a moment. "I won't come back," she said. "I won't embarrass either of us like this again." She crossed the room to the fireplace. "Part of the reason I came, whether you believe it or not, was to talk about Richard."

"Richard?" One dark eyebrow rose.

"I've been thinking about it, Andres, I know you're right; Richard has to be told. But I'd like to wait until we return to Miami."

Andres's eyes narrowed but he didn't speak.

"Dr. Olsina said Richard could be up and around by next week. I hope he'll be well enough to travel by that time." She clenched her hands together, trying to still her nervousness. "I'm going to tell him, Andres, but it would be easier to tell him after we're home."

"Easier for him or for you, Sarah?" Andres put his glass down on the coffee table and approached her. "You're not going to leave the ranch until he knows the truth," he said. "I want to know you've told him, then *I* want to talk to him."

Sarah looked into his hard, cold eyes. "Please try to understand how I feel," she said.

Andres shook his head. "Richard has to be told, the sooner the better. You've put it off long enough, Sarah. Tell him this weekend. If you don't, I will. And that's not a threat, Sarah, it's a promise."

She looked at him, this man in whose arms she'd lain only a short time ago, this man who had kissed her lips and whispered her name in the darkness of the night. There was no sympathy in his cave-black eyes.

* * *

Sarah put it off until Sunday night. Richard had managed to hobble, with the aid of new crutches, to the table for Sunday afternoon dinner. Andres had looked at Sarah; she'd looked away.

After dinner he helped Richard out onto the patio and when Doña Teresa and Silvia joined them he came back to Sarah in the dining room. "Tonight," he said. "Or tomorrow I'll tell him."

When the air began to grow chill Doña Teresa said, "You look tired, Rico. I think you've been up long enough. Let me call Andres to help you back to your room."

"Okay," Richard said good-naturedly. "Silvia and I can watch television."

"Not tonight. I . . . I'd like to talk to you." Sarah glanced at Teresa and saw the older woman tense.

Richard shrugged. "Sure, Mom." He grinned at Silvia. "See you in the morning?"

"I'm going riding early, Rico. But I'll see you as soon as I get back. I wish you were well. We could have so much fun now that summer school's over."

"I'll be all right in another week. We can go riding then."

"After you discuss it with Dr. Olsina," Sarah said. She stood up as Andres came out to the patio. He handed her Richard's crutches and picked the boy up.

"Hey, I can walk," Richard protested. "I'm not a baby."

"No, but you're tired. And if you're tired, your leg is tired," Andres said. He carried Richard down the corridor to his room and helped him into bed. "I'll see you tomorrow," he told him, then hesitating added, "I'll be staying at the house tonight, Rico. If you want anything, if you want to talk or anything, send one of the maids for me." He glanced at Sarah and without a word to her went out and closed the door behind him.

"What was that all about?" Richard leaned back against the pillows and with a sigh said, "I guess it does feel pretty good to lie down." He patted the bed next to him. "What's up, Mom? What do you want to talk about?"

"Us." Sarah took a deep breath. "You and me. Your father."

"My father?" Richard looked puzzled. "You haven't talked about him in a long time."

"I know, sweetheart." Sarah's palms were wet and she rubbed them against the sheet. "You used to ask me about him when you were younger but you don't anymore."

"I guess because he's always been a kind of shadowy figure, somebody who's never been real to me. If you'd had a picture maybe it would have been different. I know you told me that the two of you had never gotten around to having a picture taken, but gee, you'd think his family would have had some pictures. What made you think of him now?"

"Well I..." Sarah moistened her lips. "You know I spent a month here when I was seventeen?"

"Yeah, but what's that got to do with my father?" Richard looked puzzled. "I thought you were here for two months."

"I was supposed to be but I... I left before the two months were up."

"Why?"

"I was homesick."

"Homesick! I wouldn't have thought you'd missed your folks that much. You're not close to them now."

"No, well I... That wasn't the only reason I wanted to go home, Richard."

He looked at her curiously.

"I was only two years older than you are now." She hated the defensive tone in her voice, the barely hidden plea for understanding. "Carlos was almost four years older than I was."

"Silvia's father. Did you know him pretty well?"

"Pretty well. We used to drive back and forth to Guadalajara every day. He had a beat-up Volkswagen bug, a convertible."

"No kidding? What was he like? Was he like Andres?"

Sarah shook her head. "Andres has always been more serious. Even back then, when he was in his twenties. His father was ill and a lot of the responsibility on the ranch was his. He felt responsible for Carlos too." She hesitated. "Carlos was fun, Richard. He was so handsome that all the girls at school were after him."

"Were you?"

"Yes, I . . . I guess so."

"Gee." His dark eyes widened. "Were you in love with him?"

"I thought I was. He was an exciting young man, Richard. He wasn't afraid of anything. He drove too fast, he—"

"That's terrible, isn't it? That he was killed in a car accident, I mean."

"Yes." Sarah looked down at her hands, praying for the words to tell Richard what she had to tell him.

"What happened? I mean if you liked each other and everything, why didn't you get married?"

"Carlos was already engaged to Silvia's mother. But I didn't know that. He'd never told me."

"He should have!" Richard looked upset. "That's not very nice, not leveling with a girl I mean."

"No, I guess it isn't."

"So you found out about it and you got mad and went home. Is that it?"

"Richard, I . . ."

"What is it, Mom? What are you trying to tell me?"

"Something I should have told you years ago." Sarah covered his hand with hers. "Darling, I . . . I was very young. I thought I loved Carlos and—"

"So when you found out he was engaged you went back to Chicago and you met Dad and married him and then after a while I was born." His eyes looked frightened. "That's it, isn't it, Mom?"

"No." Sarah swallowed the pain in her throat. "No, Richard, that's not it."

His face was white. "I don't understand. My father was Peter Carlson. He died before I was born, he..."

Sarah wanted to put her arms around him. Instead she said, in a voice so low he could barely hear her, "There never was a Peter Carlson, Richard. I made it up. I've... I've never been married."

Richard stared at her as he backed away, up against the pillows. "Then who was my father?" he asked in a hoarse voice. But he knew. She saw in his eyes that he knew.

"Carlos." Sarah's voice shook so hard she could barely speak. "Carlos Navarro was your father."

"I don't believe you. You're making this up. You're—"

"Darling, please." Sarah began to cry. "Please, let me tell you, Richard." Fighting for control, she reached for his hand again but he pulled it away from her and crossed his arms over his chest.

"You lied to me," he said.

Sarah waited until she could speak. "I was so young, Richard. I did what I thought was best."

"Best for who? You?" His voice was scornful.

"For both of us." Sarah waited, trying to control her voice. "I didn't want you to come to Guadalajara because I was afraid of what might happen. But I told myself I was being ridiculous, that there was one chance in ten thousand that you'd ever meet anybody by the name of Navarro. I'd forgotten what a small world it is, that there might be a student in summer school with that name.

"I was so afraid when we came here to El Camichín, Richard. I saw the expression on your face that day we came up over the crest of the hill and you looked down at the ranch for the first time. There was wonder in your eyes. It was almost as though you recognized the land." Sarah's hands tightened in her lap. "The day that you were hurt there was something about the way you moved that reminded Andres of...of your father. You do look like him, Richard. You have his eyes, his dark hair, his build. When you stood there in the ring, holding the cape, Andres knew. He knew you were Carlos's son. He wanted me to tell you the truth."

"Why?" Richard's eyes blazed with anger. "So that I'd know I was a bastard?"

Sarah recoiled as though she'd been struck. "Don't say that," she pleaded.

"It's true, isn't it?"

"No, it's not true. You're my son. I love you more than anyone or anything in the world."

"Do you? Better than you loved Carlos when you...when you..." Richard put his fists against his eyes, unable to go on.

For a long time neither of them spoke. Finally Sarah said, "I'm telling you this now because both Andres and Doña Teresa want you to—"

"Grandmother Teresa knows? *She* knows?"

"She knows and she loves you," Sarah said desperately. "Both she and Andres want you to stay here at the ranch because a part of it belongs to you."

"I don't belong here. I don't belong anywhere."

"Richard, please."

"I want to be alone. Could you just go?"

"I can't leave you like this, darling."

"Please." His young voice was hard. "I don't want to talk to you now." He put his arm over his eyes.

Sarah looked at him. She wanted to touch him, wanted to beg for his forgiveness, but he didn't speak. After a moment she said, "All right, Richard, I—"

"Rico," he said in a tight voice. "Don't call me Richard."

She closed her eyes, trying to will the pain away. "Very well. I'll see you in the morning." She got up and crossed to the door. "Whatever happened before," she said in a low voice, "has nothing to do with how much I love you. I know you're hurt and I know you're angry. But I love you, Richard...Rico. All I've ever wanted was your happiness."

When he didn't answer Sarah went out and closed the door behind her.

Chapter Twelve

Sarah slept little that night. She knew how hurt Richard was and she wanted with all her heart to help him. But she couldn't unless he talked to her. It's natural that he's upset, she told herself, but if I'm patient, if I let a little time go by, it will be all right. We've always been close. That won't change, it mustn't change. He's my life. He's all I have.

The next morning she knocked at Richard's door. When he didn't answer she opened the door. His back was to her. "Richard?" she said softly. He didn't answer.

She then went into the dining room where Teresa was alone at the table. The older woman looked at her and said, "You told him?"

"Yes, I told him."

"How did he take it?"

"Not very well. He didn't want to talk to me. He wouldn't let me touch him."

"Sarah, my dear..." Teresa's fine dark eyes were full of compassion. "It was a shock to him. Give him a few days. Rico knows you love him, that we all love him. I'll speak to him if you like. He—" She stopped as Silvia came into the room.

"Hi, Grandmother. Hi, Sarah. It's a beautiful day, isn't it? Is it okay if I go riding, Grandmother?" She helped herself to a piece of toast. "I wish Rico were well enough to go." She looked at Sarah. "Will you come with me, Sarah? It's such a nice day. We could take a picnic and ride up into the hills."

"I don't think so, Silvia, but thank you for asking."

Silvia sighed. "I might as well be back in school. With Richard stuck in his room there isn't much to do. I tried to say hello to him just now but he sort of mumbled and closed his eyes."

"He's probably tired, dear," Teresa said. "He was up for a long time yesterday. And remember, even though he's much better, his leg still gives him a lot of discomfort. It isn't pleasant for him, having to spend so much time in bed. It's enough to make anyone grouchy, I imagine."

"He wasn't grouchy yesterday." Silvia sipped her orange juice and looked dejected.

Teresa looked at Sarah, then at Silvia. And suddenly Sarah thought, she has to be told. Silvia has to be told that Richard's her half brother.

"You ride, don't you, Sarah?" Teresa asked. When Sarah nodded she said, "Why don't you go riding with Silvia? It would do you good to get away from the house for a few hours."

"But Richard . . . I don't want to leave Richard."

"I'll look in on him. Perhaps he needs time to rest today." She looked at Sarah. "I really think you should go riding with Silvia, dear."

You want me to tell her, don't you? Sarah thought. It isn't enough that I've had to tell Richard, now I have to try to explain to Silvia that Richard's her half brother. She stared down at her plate. When will this end? she wondered. When can I take my son and leave El Camichín? She picked up her coffee cup, took a sip, then summoning a smile said, "I'm not a very good rider, Silvia, but if you're willing to put up with me I'd like to go with you."

"That's wonderful." Silvia beamed. "Wait till I tell Richard we're going. He—"

"You'd better let him rest," Teresa said. "You can see him later, when you and Sarah return from your ride. Now why don't you go in the kitchen and have the cook fix a lunch? There's some cold roast beef left over from dinner last night. There's cake too, if you'd like some."

"Of course we'd like some." Silvia hugged her grandmother. "Meet you in thirty minutes, Sarah," she said as she rushed to the kitchen.

The two women were silent after Silvia left. Sarah took another sip of her coffee. When she put it down she said, "You'd like me to tell her about Richard, wouldn't you?"

"I think it would be best coming from you." Doña Teresa spoke softly. "Silvia's fond of you, Sarah."

"I wonder how fond she'll be of me after I tell her Richard's her half brother." Sarah's voice was ironic. "If my own son refuses to speak to me, how do you think Silvia will react?"

"I don't know," Doña Teresa said honestly. "I only know that she has to be told. I'll do it if you don't want to."

"No, I'll tell her." Sarah put down her napkin. "When you see Richard later will you tell him . . . tell him that Silvia and I have gone riding? He may not want to talk about what happened last night."

"I understand, Sarah. I won't mention it. If he doesn't want to talk I'll just sit with him for a while."

Sarah got up and came around the table to the older woman's chair. "You're very kind to me, kinder than I deserve. And I thank you for it."

"No, Sarah, it is I who thank you, for giving me my grandson." She patted Sarah's hand. "Now go along. You'll feel better when you get some fresh air."

* * *

Sarah did feel better. For a while she was able to close one corner of her mind and simply enjoy being out of doors. The weather in this first week of August was summer warm. Afternoon rains had turned the trees and the pasture grass green, and here in the hills wildflowers covered the ground in a variegated carpet of color.

Silvia took the lead, winding up the sometimes steep trail on her surefooted Princesa. The girl had braided her heavy black hair into a single plait that hung down the middle of her back. She wore a blue-and-white checkered shirt tucked into her jeans and scuffed leather boots. She never wore makeup—"Uncle Andres won't let me," she told Sarah—and her face this morning looked buttercup fresh. She was a pretty girl, and although Sarah had only met Maria Escobar once, it seemed to her that Silvia looked much more like her mother than her father.

They spent the morning chatting about ordinary things, school and movies, rock stars and boys. "Uncle Andres won't let me date," Silvia confided. "I can go to parties and to school things, but he won't let me go out with a boy alone. Some of my friends date so I don't know why I can't. I don't think it's fair, do you?"

"Does he say when you can date?"

"Maybe when I'm fifteen. But that's a whole seven months from now."

"Fifteen sounds pretty reasonable to me. Is there anyone you particularly like?"

Silvia frowned and shook her head. "Not really, except for Richard. He's the nicest boy I know; I'd date him if I could." She grinned at Sarah. "That would be okay, wouldn't it?"

"Silvia, I..."

"What is it, Sarah? You look funny."

"It's nothing. Watch out for that low branch. Are you hungry yet?"

"I'm starved. But let's keep going a little longer. There's a meadow up ahead, just over the crest of this hill. I thought we'd eat there."

So Sarah relaxed for a moment, grateful that she'd been able to steer the conversation away from Richard.

The high meadow, filled with hollyhock, wild roses and daisies, was the perfect place to have lunch. They tied their horses in a shady spot where they could munch the summer grasses, then spread a blanket near a grove of trees.

"Isn't this wonderful?" Silvia raised her arms above her head as she looked around her. "This is my favorite place, Sarah. It's where I come when I want to be alone. I brought Richard here before he was hurt, and now you. But you're the only two people in the whole world who've ever seen it besides me."

"It's lovely, Silvia. Thank you for bringing me." Sarah opened the picnic basket and began to set out the lunch. Roast beef sandwiches, radishes, tomatoes, apples and grapes. For dessert there were three big pieces of chocolate cake.

"This is delicious," Silvia said as she bit into her sandwich. She smiled happily at Sarah. "I'm so glad you came with me. And I'm glad we're friends." She looked suddenly shy. "I'm lonesome sometimes, so it's nice having you and Richard here. I wish you didn't have to go back, Sarah. I wish the two of you could stay forever."

"I wish we could too." Sarah took a sip of her iced tea. I'll wait until we're finished eating, she told herself. Then I'll tell her.

But after they'd eaten Silvia flopped down on her back and closed her eyes. "I'm full," she announced happily. "I may never eat again."

"Until dinnertime at least." Sarah smiled as she gathered up the picnic things.

"I'm lazy, Sarah. I just want to lie here and listen to the birds." Silvia opened her eyes and with a grin said, "Tell me a story."

"Tell you a story?"

"That's what my mother used to do when it was time for my nap." The girl closed her eyes again. "Go ahead, I'm waiting." Her lips twitched in a smile.

Sarah took a deep breath. "Once upon a time," she began, "there was a girl who lived in a cold, windy city. She didn't like the wind so one summer she came to Mexico."

"What was the girl's name?" Silvia asked sleepily.

"Sa...Sabrina."

"Where did she go in Mexico?"

"Guadalajara."

"That's nice." Silvia yawned. "What did she do there?"

"She went to school and she lived with a family on a ranch."

Silvia's eyes flew open. "Like El Camichín?"

Sarah nodded. "There were two brothers on the ranch."

"Just like *papá* and Uncle Andres?" Silvia laughed. "The story's about you, isn't it, Sarah?"

For a moment Sarah hesitated. "Would you rather I tell you something else?"

"No, I want to hear about you..." She giggled. "About Sabrina, I mean."

"The younger son's name was Adelberto and—"

"Adelberto! That's a terrible name!"

"Shh. The younger son's name was Adelberto and he was handsome and fun and charming. Sabrina liked him a lot. They used to drive back and forth to school in Guadalajara every day and she spent a lot of time alone with him and...and maybe she shouldn't have."

"Why not? Wasn't she old enough to be alone with a boy?"

"She thought she was, Silvia, but she hadn't gone out with a lot of boys and she really wasn't very experienced." Sarah hesitated. "Anyway, there was a big party on the night of Adelberto's twenty-first birthday. He and Sabrina danced and she kissed him happy birthday."

"I should think so." Silvia sat up. Her eyes were wide as she watched Sarah. "What happened then?"

Sarah pulled a blade of grass out of the ground. How can I tell her? she thought. How can I make her understand what happened?

"Go on," Silvia prodded. "What happened then?"

"Summer ended, Silvia. Sabrina had to go back where she came from."

A look of disappointment crossed Silvia's face. "Is that the end of the story?"

"No." She looked at Silvia, then away. "Sabrina was pregnant," she said.

"Preg…" The dark eyes widened with shock. "She and Adelberto…? You and *papá*?"

Sarah tried to speak and couldn't. All she could do was nod her head.

For a moment Silvia too was speechless. Then her face changed. "Oh, Sarah," she whispered, and fell forward into Sarah's arms.

"Don't cry, Silvia. Darling, please. I know how awful this is for you. How you must feel, but—"

"Awful?" Tears streaked Silvia's face. "I've wanted you to be my *something* ever since that night in the stable. And now you are, you're my aunt. Well, almost my aunt, and I sort of belong to you now."

"Silvia, I…" Sarah couldn't speak then as she clasped the girl to her. Of all the reactions she'd expected, this certainly wasn't one of them. She'd learned to love Silvia, and the thought of the girl turning away from her, as Richard had, was almost more than she could bear. Now Silvia was clinging to her, weeping on her shoulder, and telling her how glad she was because now Sarah could stay at El Camichín forever.

"Does Grandmother know?" Silvia said when she sat back and wiped her eyes.

"Yes, dear."

"How does she feel about it?"

"Happy, I think. She has a grandson she didn't know she had and—"

"Rico's my brother!" It was as though a light had suddenly gone on in Silvia's head. "He's my half brother!" A strange expression crossed her face. "How about that? I've got a brother!"

Sarah sighed with relief. She'd expected Silvia to be appalled by the fact that she had a half brother, but instead the girl seemed overjoyed.

Now as Silvia lay down again, looking up at the sky, she said, "Come lie beside me, Sarah." For a long time she didn't speak and then she said, "Tell me about my father. Did you love him?"

Sarah held her breath. Then she leaned on her elbow and smiling down at Silvia said, "Yes, I loved him. He was a dear and wonderful young man. I'll never forget him, Silvia."

"Did you...did you tell him you were...you know?"

"No, dear." Sarah smoothed the damp hair back off Silvia's forehead. "Your father and I had a lovely summer, Silvia. But summer doesn't last forever.

When it was over and I had gone he saw your mother and knew that it was her he loved.''

"But that doesn't seem fair, Sarah. He had *mamá* and you didn't have anybody."

"I had Richard. I loved him and we...we lived happily ever after."

"Does he know? About *papá* being his father?"

Sarah nodded.

"What did he say?"

"It was a shock, Silvia. He didn't say very much."

"Would it be okay if I told him I knew?"

"Yes, I think so."

"Then I'll tell him." As though relieved that everything had been settled, Silvia sat up and helped herself to another piece of cake.

It was late that afternoon when, tired but content, Sarah and Silvia returned to the ranch. Sarah bathed and changed, then went to see Richard. He was sitting up in bed, a pillow under his bad leg.

"Hi." Sarah kissed his forehead. "How's the leg today?"

"Okay." He switched on the television.

"Silvia and I went horseback riding. I bet I'll be sore tomorrow. It's been a long time since I've ridden."

"I suppose you told her."

"Yes, Richard, I told her."

He turned up the volume on the television.

"Please don't do that." Sarah reached for the remote control and turned down the sound. In a gentle voice she said, "We have to talk. I'm your mother, Richard, I love you."

"You want to tell me some more about my father?"

"Yes, if you want me to."

"And about all the other men?"

Sarah stared at him. Her face paled. "What...what do you mean?"

"He wasn't the only one, was he? There must have been others. How can you be sure Carlos Navarro was my father? How—?"

But before he could go on Sarah turned and ran out of the room. She stood in the corridor, leaning against the wall, unable to move, to think or to feel, her hand over her mouth to still a terrible cry of despair.

She didn't see Andres until he spoke her name, but when he put his hand on her shoulder she turned away from him, doubling over as though she were in pain.

"Sarah, what is it?"

She shook her head, unable to answer.

Andres stared down at her, then picked her up and carried her down the hall to her room. When he'd laid her on the bed he said, "What is it, Sarah? Are you ill?"

She shook her head and turned away from him, knees drawn up, arms across her chest as though to protect herself.

Andres sat down next to her. He put his hand on her forehead, he looked at her anguished face. "Tell me," he said.

"No!"

The cry chilled him. For the first time since he had discovered the truth about Richard he began to sense how hard this had been on Sarah. He didn't know what had happened to trigger this terrible grief, but he knew it had something to do with the boy.

He went into the bathroom, wet a washcloth and brought it back so that he could wipe her face. She kept her eyes closed and refused to look at him.

When he put the cloth aside he said, "Tell me what happened, Sarah." He put his hand on her shoulder. I want you, Sarah, he wanted to say. Come live with me. Be my love. The past doesn't matter, all that's important is today and tomorrow and all the tomorrows we can share together.

But because he couldn't say those things he said, "Was it Silvia? I know you went riding with her today. Did you tell her about Richard? Did she say something to hurt you?"

"No. She said she'd wanted me to be her 'something' and now I was and she..." She sat up. "Silvia was fine," she said.

"It was Richard then. What did he say to hurt you this way?"

"He said..." Her eyes looked lost and empty. "He's been so hurt, Andres. I don't blame him. I—"

"What did he say?"

The empty eyes filled with pain. "He asked me about . . . about all the other men. He asked me how I could be sure that Carlos really was his father. How . . ." She looked at Andres. "That's the way you think too, isn't it? That's why you don't want to . . ." She turned away from him. "You feel just like Richard does, Andres. You think there were others, too."

She covered her face with her hands, resisting when Andres tried to pull her into his arms.

"Stop it," he said. "I know there wasn't anybody but Carlos. I know Richard's his son. If it had been anybody else . . ." He let the sentence hang in the air.

"Let me go," Sarah said in a tired voice.

When he did she lay down and, turning away from him again, closed her eyes.

Andres reached out to touch her, then stopped. Without a word he got up and left the room.

Chapter Thirteen

How dare you speak to your mother that way?"
Andres stared down at the boy on the bed. "How dare
you?"

Richard's eyes widened. He swallowed, then with
forced bravado said, "It's none of your damn business."

"Isn't it? I'm your uncle, Richard. You use that
tone of voice to me again and I'll yank you right up
out of your bed."

"Yeah? And then what?"

"You'll regret ever insulting her." Andres took another step forward.

Richard held his hands in front of him. "Okay,

okay. I'm sorry. But I meant it. It isn't any of your business and you're not my uncle."

"The hell I'm not! Whether you like it or not, you *are* my brother's son. You look like him, you're built like him, you even move like him. That day in the bullring it was as though I was looking at him at your age. You're a Navarro all right, but you certainly aren't acting like one."

"What do you mean?" Richard asked angrily.

"The men of our family have always prided themselves on being gentlemen. What you did to your mother this afternoon was unforgivable. I don't know how she can forgive you but she will because she loves you."

"She loves everybody!"

Andres stared down at the boy, almost too angry to speak. Then he noticed that there were tears in Richard's eyes.

For a moment man and boy stared at each other. Then Andres pulled up a chair beside the bed. Richard looked at him warily.

"You and your mother usually get along all right?" Andres forced himself to speak calmly. "I mean before you found out about your father?"

Richard nodded. "We get along."

Andres tried to choose his words carefully because up to now Sarah had been the most important person in Richard's life. Like most young men he'd very likely thought his mother immune to any feeling of desire. Sarah was his mother, she'd always been there for him.

His father had only been a remote figure who had come briefly into his mother's life. Now Richard had suddenly discovered that Sarah was a woman of flesh and blood. She'd loved someone real, not just a shadowy figure. She'd made love to a man who'd been more than a cipher.

Sarah's news had come as a terrible shock to Richard. Andres understood that, but he also understood Sarah's grief. He had made her confess her relationship with Carlos. She had lost a great deal in her life; she mustn't lose her son's love.

"Go to many parties?" Andres asked casually.

"Sure." Richard looked at him, startled by the sudden change in topic.

"You take girls out?"

"Yeah, naturally I take girls out."

"Your mother's all right about it? She lets you go out? Doesn't cross-examine you every time you step out of the house?"

"No, she says I'm old enough to have some sense. She said if I ever drank or used drugs she'd shoot my kneecaps off." A reluctant grin crossed Richard's face. "I believed her so I never touched any of that stuff."

"Good for you. How do you get along with your grandparents?"

"Okay I guess. We don't see much of them because we live in Miami and they're in Chicago."

"You think that's the only reason you don't see them?"

"No, not exactly." Richard shifted in the bed and adjusted the pillow under his leg. "They're really strange, you know? Like stiff and proper. They're always correcting Mom and telling her she doesn't dress right or that she should be stricter with me. Stuff like that."

"How'd you like to live with them all the time?"

"No way!"

Andres got up and went to the dresser. "Want a glass of juice?" he asked. Richard nodded and Andres poured two glasses of apple juice. When he sat down again he handed a glass to Richard, then touched his to it and said, *"Salud."* He took a drink, then set the glass on the bedside table.

"How do you think it might have been for your mom, growing up with people like that?"

Richard looked uncomfortable. "Not so hot I guess."

"I guess not." Andres hesitated. "When your mother first came here to El Camichín she'd never been away from home before, Rico. She was far away from her parents and for the first time in her life she was free. That must have been pretty exciting for her." He took another sip of the juice. "Your mother's a pretty woman, Rico. At seventeen she was...heart-breakingly lovely. But she was very naive and unsure of herself. I imagine you know more about life at fifteen than your mother did at seventeen."

Andres leaned forward in his chair. "Your mother didn't have a chance, Rico. Carlos zeroed in on her like a hawk circling a mouse. Yes, they made love, they shouldn't have but they were young and he couldn't handle his emotions. And your mother got pregnant.''

"She didn't tell my . . . your brother?"

"No, I guess she felt that the responsibility was hers. And that was pretty damn brave of her. Your grand-parents didn't help her and for a long time, before she went to live with her aunt, I imagine she felt scared and lonely. But she toughed it out, Richard, she had you and loved you and raised you.''

Tears stood out in Richard's eyes now, but Andres didn't stop. He couldn't spare the boy; he wouldn't spare himself. "I made her tell you," he said. "I told her that if she didn't I would. I've been just as hard on her as you've been, Rico, but for different reasons."

Andres got up abruptly and went to stand by the window. He waited until he heard Richard blow his nose before he turned back to the bed. "I made your mother tell you because as Carlos's son El Camichín is partly yours.''

Richard sat up straight, his mouth half open as he stared at Andres. "What . . . what do you mean?"

"You're a Navarro, Carlos's son. Your grand-mother and I want you to stay here on the ranch."

"Here? With you and Grandmother Teresa and Silvia?''

Andres nodded. "This is your home, Rico. It's where you belong."

"What . . . what about school?"

"There are several private academies in Guadalajara. Your Spanish is good so you shouldn't have any trouble. We could enroll you this fall. You like it here, don't you?"

"I like it all right. It's the greatest place in the world." He looked up at Andres. "What about Mom?"

"She'd want to go back to Miami, I imagine. You'd see her on school vacations, summers, whenever you like. She'd be welcome to visit."

She'd be welcome to visit. It's as though you were talking about a stranger, Andres thought, someone you barely know. Not someone you... But it was Richard he had to think about. The boy had a future here at El Camichín. This was where he belonged. And what about Sarah? Where does Sarah belong? asked a small voice in his head.

"I want you to think about it, Rico," Andres said. "Nobody's going to force you to do anything. I wanted you to know how your grandmother and I feel." He put his hand on Richard's shoulder. "We're your people and we love you. We want you to stay with us, but it has to be your decision. You think about it, all right?"

"Yes, sir."

"Try *Tío* Andres, will you?"

Richard blushed. "Okay."

"I saw your mother in the hall a little while ago, Rico. She feels pretty bad. I'd like you to tell her you're sorry and make it up with her."

"Right now?"

"Right now. Do you need any help with your crutches?"

"No, I . . . I can manage."

"Get to it then."

"Yes, sir. I mean *Tío*."

"Good. I'll see you later. We'll talk some more if you want to."

"I'd like to know more about my father."

Andres nodded. "Tonight," he said.

Sarah heard the thump of crutches in the tile corridor outside her room. There was a knock, then Richard said, "Mom, may I come in?"

Sarah wiped the tears away with her fingertips and tried to smooth her tousled hair. "Just a minute." A minute to take a deep breath and get a grip on herself before she said, "Yes, Richard, come in," and hurried across the room to help him.

He didn't speak until he was in the room. When he looked at her he said, "You've been crying."

"I'm all right now."

His Adam's apple bobbed as he swallowed hard. "I'm sorry I said those things," he blurted. "I didn't mean to, Mom. I didn't mean any of that stuff I said."

"I know."

"I don't suppose you can ever forgive me."

"Of course I can forgive you, if you can forgive me." Sarah tried to put her arms around him but the crutches were in the way. She was crying again but through her tears she said, "Come sit down so I can give you a hug." And when he did they put their arms around each other and it was all right again.

Sarah sat beside him. "I'm sorry I lied to you, Richard. I did it because I wanted to protect you, and maybe because I wanted to protect me too. Today it's all right for a single woman to have a child, but it wasn't fifteen years ago. If my parents had been a little more understanding I might have done things differently."

"Andres told me they didn't help you."

"You've talked to Andres?"

"Yeah. He came to my room right after you left. He was so mad he scared the hell out of me." There was a touch of admiration in Richard's voice. "He's one tough guy. He tells you to do something you know you'd better do it. I really like him."

"You *like* him?"

"Yeah, he's tough but underneath you get this feeling of strength. Like here's a guy who'll never let you down." He looked at Sarah. "He asked me to call him Uncle Andres, and he told me that he and Grandmother Teresa want me to stay here. He said this was my home and that it's where I should be."

"How do you feel about that, Richard?"

"I don't know," he said honestly. "I love it here, I have right from the very first day. But I've always lived in Miami. There's school and football..." He hesitated. "It's a tough decision."

"I know it is, Richard."

"Besides, I'd be here and you'd be in Miami. I know I'm not a little kid or anything, but I'd miss you. Andres said I could visit you of course. And you could visit here." He looked at her, his dark eyes full of questions. "What do you think, Mom?"

Sarah touched his hair. "It has to be your decision, Richard."

He nodded. "I guess so."

"But you don't have to decide right away, you've got plenty of time before your leg heals and it's time to leave. School doesn't start until the first week in September, you'll have until then."

"Andres said there are a lot of private academies in Guadalajara. I'll go to school there—if I stay, I mean. Andres said that I belong here, that El Camichín is partly mine. Can you imagine that, Mom? Part of all this belongs to me."

Sarah listened and smiled and said all of the right things, knowing in her heart that Richard had already decided.

Two weeks went by. Richard talked to Sarah a lot about his father. He wanted to know everything about Carlos. What was he like? What did he like to do? Was he a good rider? A good student? His questions were endless.

Richard spent a lot of time with his grandmother, asking her the same questions he asked Sarah. Now that he had accepted the fact that Carlos had been his father, he couldn't stop talking about him. Doña Te-

resa was happier than she'd been since Carlos's death.
She answered all of Richard's questions, showed him
every picture that had ever been taken of Carlos, and
delighted in being with the boy.

But it was with Andres that Richard, once he was
able to get around, spent most of his time. Andres
gave him a gentle mare, and with Dr. Olsina's ap-
proval, took the boy riding every day. Silvia went with
them as often as her grandmother would let her. She'd
been shy around Richard for the first few days after
she found out he was her half brother, but that had
passed and they were now closer than ever. Silvia loved
riding up into the hills with Richard and Andres, but
when the rides turned into long explanations about
every operation of the ranch she decided to stay at
home.

Richard, however, listened to everything Andres had
to say. The older man was patient with him. He took
Richard out in the pasture to ride among the brave
bulls, assuring Richard that bulls only attacked when
they were separated from the herd. He told him about
bloodlines and breeding, everything that went into the
raising of bulls.

Little by little, unaware that it was happening, a
strong bond developed between Andres and Richard—or Rico, as he now preferred to be called.

"You don't mind, do you, Mom?" he'd asked
Sarah. "Rico Navarro. It sounds good, doesn't it?
Andres said that if I wanted to, if it was okay with you,

he'd attend to legally changing my name. I'd like to, if you don't mind."

"I don't mind," Sarah had said. "It's a good name."

Every day Richard grew further and further away from her and there wasn't anything she could do, even if she wanted to. His face glowed with happiness and when he talked to her his conversation was punctuated with, "*Tío* Andres says . . ." It was happening, sooner than Sarah had ever imagined it would. She was losing her son.

It was a strange time for Andres, an exciting time. He'd never had children of his own. After Carlos and Maria had been killed he'd tried to be a surrogate father to Silvia, but she was a girl and most of the responsibility of raising her went to his mother. He'd been careful with Silvia because she was a girl. He worried that she might fall when she rode Princesa. He worried if anyone else drove her to and from school. He loved her but he was so concerned about doing the right thing that he never relaxed and enjoyed being with her.

It was different with Richard, perhaps because Richard was older and tougher. He had a lot of Carlos in him but he was more serious than Carlos had ever been. Carlos had been a hell-raiser, game for anything, ready to take on any challenge as long as it was exciting. He had a fast mind and a quick wit. You couldn't rely on him to mend a fence, but if an animal was sick Carlos took care of it with sure and tender hands.

He'd been a good husband to Maria Escobar. He'd loved their baby when it was born and spent a lot of time with Silvia as she was growing up. But he drank too much and he drove too fast, and in the end it had killed him.

Andres told Richard only the good things about his father. He's like him, Andres thought, and yet he isn't like him. He's stronger than Carlos, more responsible at fifteen than Carlos had been at twenty-five.

A lot of that strength, Andres knew, came from Sarah. She'd done a remarkable job with the boy, raising him alone. It was going to be difficult for her when she had to leave him.

Andres didn't try to influence Richard in the decision the boy had to make, he only showed him what would be his and explained what it would be like if Richard decided to stay—and tried to put the thought of how Sarah would feel out of his mind.

Andres hadn't seen much of her these past two weeks. He told himself it was because he was busy with the ranch and with Richard, but he knew that wasn't the only reason. At the end of August, as soon as Richard was completely well, Sarah would leave El Camichín—with or without her son. If he saw her again it would be for a week or two in the summer when she came to visit Richard. Now it was as though he were preparing himself for the separation that was to come.

For fifteen years the thought of Sarah had stayed in a small corner of his mind. There were so many nights after she left the ranch that he'd lain awake thinking about her; nights when he remembered what it had been like that day on the hill when he'd held her in his arms. He remembered the feel of her mouth, so soft and yielding against his. He had dreamed of what it would be like to hold her again. Then the dream had become a reality and it had been more than he had ever imagined lovemaking could be. But God forgive him, he'd hated himself for having touched her, and a part of him hated her for letting him.

Sarah, Andres thought as night after night he stood at his window, looking across the patio to her room. He wanted to go to her more times than he could count. I could slip into her room, he told himself. No one would see me. I could hold her, there in her bed and... The same bed, he'd think then. The bed where Carlos had taken her. He couldn't do that; it was too late for him. He and Sarah could never have more than what they'd already had.

But he would have her son. Sarah's son, a part of her. A boy he could raise as his own.

Chapter Fourteen

The August sun felt warm on Sarah's face. She closed her eyes and leaned back in the lounge chair, listening to the soft splatter of water in the stone fountain. She'd felt very alone these past two weeks. Now that Richard's leg was better he spent every day with Andres, and when he wasn't with Andres he was with Silvia or his grandmother.

There are so many things he has to find out about the family, Sarah told herself. He's just discovering who he is and what his father was like. She understood, but there were times when she felt left out and alone, for it seemed to her that Richard had already begun to move away.

It would have been the same at home, Sarah told herself. Richard's fifteen. In two more years he'll be ready for college, and after that for a job and later on a family of his own. I can't keep him with me forever, she thought, I never expected that I would. But she'd known that however old Richard was he'd still have been a part of her life, as she would always have been a part of his. That wouldn't be true if he stayed here at El Camichín. Here, he'd belong to the Navarros and Sarah would only be a sometime visitor.

So Sarah watched and waited, knowing that when Richard finally reached a conscious decision he would tell her. Until he did, the waiting was hard.

She and Andres had not spoken intimately since the day he'd found her crying in the corridor. In a curious way Sarah mourned for him just as she mourned over her coming loss of Richard. She knew that she loved Andres, that she'd loved him since that long-ago day on the hill overlooking El Camichín when he'd told her of Carlos's engagement to Maria Escobar. He'd been harsh and unkind that day, but then he'd held her and kissed her and there'd been no harshness in his embrace. She'd thought of him for fifteen years and when at last she'd seen him it had been as though time had stood still; she'd been seventeen again, trembling on the edge of love, as afraid as she'd been before.

For a little while Sarah had almost allowed herself to believe that Andres might some day love her—but that was before he'd learned the truth about Carlos.

Finally, because she could not bear to be alone with her thoughts, Sarah left the patio and wandered down to the stable. She liked the smell of horses, hay and leather saddles. Andres had kissed her here, he had touched her and almost made love to her. The thought of Carlos had stopped him.

Sarah took a carrot out of the pocket of her dress and fed it to Princesa. "Good old girl," she said as she rubbed the mare's smooth black nose.

She was still by Princesa's stall when Richard and Andres rode up.

"Hi, Mom," Richard said. "What are you doing?"

"Just talking to Princesa." Sarah glanced up at Andres, then back to Richard. "Did the two of you have a good ride?"

"Yeah, we rode out to the north pasture. Just beyond it there's a piece of land that we're going to seed for clover. We..." He glanced at Andres.

"How'd you like to take care of the horses?" Andres dismounted and loosened his saddle cinch. "There's something I want to check on up at the house."

"Sure thing," Richard said.

Andres nodded at Sarah, then with a meaningful look at Richard he left the stable.

"It was a nice day for a ride." Sarah rubbed the mare's nose and tried not to look at her son.

"Yeah." He cleared his throat. "Mom, I...I guess we need to talk."

"All right, Richard." Sarah summoned a smile. "Can I help you with the horses?"

"No, that's okay. I know how. Uncle Andres showed me." He looked at her, then away as he heaved one of the saddles over a stall railing. "I guess you've been wondering what I've decided, about whether or not I'm going to stay here I mean."

"Yes, I've been wondering." But Sarah knew. She'd realized it the moment Richard had ridden into the stable with Andres.

"You know I love you and everything."

"I know, Richard."

"And I like Miami okay, the beach and fishing and all that stuff, but . . ."

"You'd rather be here. That's it, isn't it, Richard?"

He looked embarrassed. "Yeah, Mom. That's it. I hope you're not mad."

"Of course I'm not mad." Sarah handed him the curry brush. "If I were you I'd probably do exactly the same thing. El Camichín is a wonderful place. Your grandmother and Silvia and . . . and Andres love you. You'll be happy here with them."

"I know, Mom, but you know I'll miss you."

"Of course I know that, darling. I'll miss you too. But we'll write and we'll talk on the phone."

"And you'll come for Christmas?"

"I . . . I don't think I can, Richard. I've taken so much time off this summer."

"But next summer? You'll come next summer?"

"Of course." Sarah kissed him. "You smell horsey," she said. "It's a nice smell."

His dark eyes searched hers. "You're not mad at me?"

"No, I'm not mad. You're almost a man, Richard. You had a tough decision to make and you made it." Sarah's eyes misted. "But I'm going to miss you."

"I'll miss you too."

"I'd better get back now. I told your grandmother I'd show the cook how to make crepes." Sarah ruffled his hair and said, "See you at dinner." Then she hurried out of the barn before he could see that she was crying.

Andres watched the two of them that night at dinner. Richard was nervous and he kept stealing troubled glances at his mother as if to assure himself she wasn't angry. Andres didn't think she was, though she was quiet. She spoke when she was spoken to and summoned a smile when the conversation called for one. She wore more makeup tonight and he suspected that was to hide the fact that she'd been crying. She was wearing a simple ivory linen dress with a single strand of coral around her throat. She looks beautiful, Andres thought. She looks lost.

He was only half aware of the conversation going on about him when his mother said, "If you'll excuse me, I'd like to lie down."

"Aren't you feeling well, Mother?" Andres asked as he rose to help her out of her chair.

"I'm a little tired, dear. That's all."

"Let me take you to your room."

"No, but thank you. Finish your dinner." She rested her hand on Sarah's shoulder for a minute. "You might look in on me before you go to bed."

"Of course, Doña Teresa. Perhaps you'd feel like a cup of tea then."

"Perhaps."

"Is Grandmother sick?" Silvia said when Teresa had left the room.

"I don't think so," Andres said. "We have to remember that she's getting older and she tires easily. She'll feel better in the morning. Why don't you look in on her after dinner?"

"I will." Silvia looked relieved. "Where did you and Rico ride today?"

The conversation about the ranch flowed on around Sarah. It didn't concern her because she knew nothing about the ranch operation, but it was obvious that Richard did. He asked questions and he made suggestions. Andres listened to him, explained, and often nodded in agreement. It struck Sarah suddenly that Richard had already taken his first step away from her. He'd already become a part of this land. In a few years he'd be more at ease in Mexico than in his own country. His ties would be here with his Mexican family.

When finally dinner was over Sarah slipped a shawl over her shoulders and escaped onto the patio. Richard had gone with Silvia to check on Teresa; she didn't know where Andres was.

The air was still, and except for the pleasant splash of water in the fountain and the occasional call of a night bird, everything was quiet. Moving closer to the fountain, Sarah sat on the edge and dipped her fingers in the water, then touched the cool wetness to her cheeks. For a long time she stared down into the fountain.

When she looked up she saw Andres at the edge of the garden. As he came closer Sarah tightened the shawl around her shoulders.

"I need to talk to you." He put one foot up on the fountain, close to her hip. "Did Richard speak to you this afternoon?"

"Yes. You told him to, didn't you?" She couldn't keep the bitterness out of her voice.

"I thought it was time. Richard reached his decision several days ago but he was afraid to tell you. It was difficult for him." Andres looked down at her. "What will you do now?"

"Go home." Sarah didn't look at him as she trailed her fingers through the water. "I'll call the airline in the morning. It's Wednesday, I'd like to leave by the end of the week."

Three days, Andres thought. He touched Sarah's shoulder and felt her tremble. "Richard's going to be all right," he said. "I won't let anything happen to him."

"I know that."

"Perhaps you could come back for Christmas."

"I don't think so."

"Look, I know this is difficult for you. I wish things could have been different. I—"

"Uncle Andres!" Silvia cried from the door. "Uncle Andres, come quick! It's Grandmother. Something's the matter with her."

He jumped up and ran to the house, Sarah a step behind him. "Call Dr. Olsina," he told her. "Tell him to come now, right now!"

Sarah called. A nurse said Dr. Olsina wasn't in but that if it was an emergency she could get in touch with him.

"It's Señora Navarro," Sarah said. "Please have him come immediately."

"He'll be here," she told Silvia when she put the phone down. She put her arms around the girl. "It's going to be all right. Dr. Olsina will know what to do. Will you wait here and bring him in? I want to see if I can do anything for your grandmother."

Silvia nodded. "I'm so scared, Sarah," she whispered. "What if something happens to Grandmother?"

"Nothing's going to happen to her, Silvia." She looked up and saw Richard coming toward them. "How is she?" Sarah asked. "What happened?"

"I don't know, Mom. She looked awfully tired and sort of white. We were talking and then all of a sudden she grabbed her chest and said, 'Get Andres.' Then she . . . I guess she fainted." He looked frightened. "Is she going to be all right, Mom?"

"I hope so, Richard. I've called the doctor. He'll be here soon." She kissed both of them, then hurried down the corridor to Doña Teresa's room.

Andres's face was almost as white as his mother's. "How is she?" Sarah whispered as she drew close to the bed.

"She's conscious now. She..."

"Don't whisper." Teresa's eyelids fluttered.

"Dr. Olsina's on his way." Sarah took the older woman's hand.

"I don't want to go to the hospital." Teresa's hand tightened on Sarah's. "I want to be here with my family."

"We'll wait to see what Olsina says." Andres looked at Sarah, his face tight with worry. "We want what's best for you, *madre*."

"El Camichín is best for me." Teresa closed her eyes and held onto Sarah's hand. When the doctor arrived he asked Sarah and Andres to leave him alone with Teresa for a few moments.

"She looks so weak," Andres said as he closed his eyes and leaned against the wall.

"Dr. Olsina will know what to do," Sarah said with more assurance than she felt. Then she didn't speak, simply waiting, as Andres did, for the doctor to come out of Doña Teresa's room.

When he did he motioned them farther down the hall. "It's not a heart attack, Andres," he said.

"That's what I was afraid of."

"Then what is it?"

"She's old and her heart's tired. There's not much we can do about that except make sure that she takes her medicine and that she rests as much as possible. I want her to stay in bed for four or five days. When she gets up she'll have to take it easy. I don't want her doing anything strenuous or getting upset because her heart simply won't take it."

He hesitated, looking from Sarah to Andres. "I'd prefer she have a full-time nurse but when I suggested it she said she wouldn't hear of it. I overruled her. At least for the next week I want a registered nurse with her. After that perhaps Señora Carlson and Silvia can take care of her."

"But I . . ." Sarah glanced at Andres, then away. "Yes, of course, Dr. Olsina. I'm sure between the two of us we can manage."

"Good. Now if you'll let me use your phone, Andres, I'll call Amelia Sanchez. She's just off a case and I'm sure she'll be willing to come. You keep her here for at least a week, longer if your mother will agree."

When Olsina hurried off to the telephone Andres said, "I don't expect you to take care of my mother, Sarah. But if you could stay for another few days—just until she's feeling better—I'd appreciate it. I know I haven't any right to ask, but I'm afraid she'd be upset if you left now."

"I have no intention of leaving when she's ill." Sarah's voice was calm but inside she was torn with emotion. It would be torture to stay here and watch Richard growing further and further away from her;

to be so close to Andres, loving him, wanting him....
But she mustn't think about anything else now except
Teresa. That must be her main concern for the next
few days.

Dr. Olsina came every day. "She's making pro-
gress," he told Andres when four days had passed.
"But it's slow. I think that as much as she resisted
having a nurse she's glad that Sanchez is here. She tells
me you've been sleeping in your mother's room at
night."

"The nurse can't be on duty twenty-four hours a
day. I want to be close by in case Mother needs me."

Olsina clapped Andres on the shoulder. "I'm pretty
sure your mother's going to be all right now. I'll keep
a close eye on her, don't worry. All I want to caution
you about is not having her get upset. That would be
the worst thing in the world for her now. If I were you
I'd go along with whatever she says." The doctor
looked thoughtful. "How soon must Señora Carlson
return to the United States?"

"In a few days I imagine," Andres said. "She has
to get back to her job."

"Pity. Your mother's fond of her." He snapped his
bag shut. "Well, I'll be on my way. See you tomorrow."

In a few days. Andres ran a tired hand over his face.
In a few days he would drive Sarah to the airport in
Guadalajara and put her on a plane. Goodbye, Sarah,
thank you for being so kind to my mother. Thank you

for your son. Thank you for whispering my name in the darkness of the night. He closed his eyes, trying to will away the anguish of his thoughts.

On the sixth day of her illness Teresa Navarro called for her son.

"Close the door," she said when Andres came in. "Bring a chair close to the bed so we can talk."

She looks so frail, Andres thought with alarm, so much older than she looked only a week ago. It frightened him because for the first time in his life he realized that his mother might die.

But he tried to keep the fear out of his voice as he took her hand and said, "What is it, *mamacita*? What's troubling you?"

"You're troubling me, Andres. You and Sarah and Richard."

His dark brows came together in a questioning frown. "But why? Everything's been settled. Richard's going to stay here with us. He's going to be a Navarro."

"And Sarah? What's going to happen to her?"

"She'll go back to Miami, of course." Andres avoided his mother's eyes.

"Just like that, eh? *Muy bien*, Sarah, you have given us your son. Now it is time for you to leave." Teresa's eyes, so much like Andres's, pierced him. "Carlos took her girlhood; now we have taken her son. What have we given her in return, Andres? The privilege of taking care of me? An invitation to visit occasionally?''

"Sarah has her own life," Andres said. "She has friends, a job. I'm sure she's content living the way she does."

"You're sure, are you?" Teresa sat up straighter in bed. "Well I'm not, Andres. I think when she leaves here Sarah will go back to a lonely house. Richard is her life, he—''

"But he's a Navarro. He belongs here, you said so yourself."

"Yes, Andres, he belongs here. So does Sarah."

Andres stared at her. His mother met his look squarely and it was he who turned away first.

"I don't want her to go, Andres. I want Sarah to stay here with her son. I want her to be a part of our family, a Navarro."

"But she's not a Navarro, Mother."

Teresa's hand tightened on his. "She would be if you married her."

Andres stared at his mother, his eyes wide with shock. "You want me to marry Sarah?"

"I want you to keep her here and I think that's the only way you can." Teresa rested for a moment, then said, "Sarah's a lovely girl, Andres. I can't believe that what I'm asking you to do will be a sacrifice. I've seen the way the two of you look at each other. I don't know whether it's love you feel, but it's something. Perhaps it's enough to build a marriage on. I don't know. All I know is that our Carlos turned Sarah's life around. She had to leave her parents' home, she had to raise Richard alone. Now we've taken him away from her and I . . . I don't think I can live with that."

"Mother, I—"

"I want her to stay, Andres. I want you to make her stay."

Andres didn't know what to say. He was astounded that his mother would ask...no, not ask, *demand* such a thing. Sarah would never agree to marry him...even if he agreed to ask her.

Teresa closed her eyes. "I want to rest now," she said. "Please think about what I said, Andres. It's important to me, son."

"But I . . ." Andres hesitated, struck again by how frail she looked and the lines in her face that he hadn't seen before. The blue-veined hand that rested in his was pale and thin. He brought it to his lips and kissed it. "I'll see you in the morning," he said.

When he went out he beckoned to Amelia Sanchez. "Mother's resting," he told her. "If she wakes later and needs anything, please call me."

"I will, *señor.*"

The house was quiet when Andres went out to the patio. In his mind's eye he could still see Sarah as she had been on the night his mother was taken ill, sitting beside the fountain, trailing her fingers through the water.

He shook his head as though trying to clear it. What his mother had asked was impossible. Marry Sarah? No, it wouldn't work, not for either of them. Sarah would never agree to it. And if she did? Andres thought of the times he'd made love to her. He remembered how she had responded, the way she'd felt in his arms. She'd been warmth and sweetness. She'd given, with willing abandon, as much as she received.

Andres closed his eyes. No, he thought. A marriage wasn't based solely on a physical relationship. There had to be a lot of other things such as mutual respect and trust, forgiveness and understanding. If I married her, he thought, the memory of Carlos would intrude on our lives. He'd always be there, in the room with us, every time we made love.

Andres ran a distracted hand through his hair as he stared into the darkness. I want Sarah, he thought. I want to sleep next to her every night for the rest of my life. But I don't know if I can ever love her as she deserves to be loved, completely, without any reservations.

What his mother had asked of him was impossible. And yet... Andres closed his eyes. God help me, he thought. What am I going to do?

Finally, when the night grew cold, he went in and took up his lonely vigil beside his mother's bed.

Chapter Fifteen

Sarah sat with Teresa most of the morning. When Dr. Olsina came in the afternoon he said, "She's not recovering as fast as I expected, Andres."

"Isn't there something we can do?" Andres asked.

"Just let her rest. We'll keep a close eye on her. I'm sure she'll come around."

Several days went by and Teresa didn't improve. Andres left the house only to check on the men and attend to what had to be taken care of. Silvia tiptoed around the house, her face pinched and frightened, even though Sarah did her best to reassure her.

Richard was frightened too. "It's terrible, Mom," he told Sarah. "I've just found out that she's my grandmother and now she..." He couldn't go on.

"She's not going to die," Sarah said. "Not for a long time, Richard." She touched the side of his face. "Your grandmother's just tired, honey. She's not going to be able to do the things she used to do, but if we take good care of her I'm sure she's going to improve."

"What about you, Mom? You're going to have to leave soon, aren't you?"

"Not until your grandmother's better, Richard."

Sarah telephoned her boss. He muttered a few choice words that were distinctly Cuban and finally told her to take as long as she had to, but that the minute things settled down in Mexico he wanted her back.

On the evening of the same day that Sarah had telephoned her boss, Andres knocked at her bedroom door.

"I need to talk to you," he said. "But not here. Let's go out for a drink."

"I was about to go to bed."

"It's important, Sarah."

She looked at him, wondering what could be so important that it had to be discussed that very moment. Then she nodded and said, "I'll be just a few minutes."

"I'll wait for you out on the patio."

Quickly Sarah slipped into a summer dress of pale apricot cotton, ran a brush through her hair and added a touch of color to her lips. She had no idea what Andres wanted to see her about. Perhaps this was to be a formal goodbye. Perhaps he planned to say, My mother's improving, Sarah. There's no need for you to stay. Adios, *sayonara*, and goodbye. We don't need you here anymore.

She looked at herself in the mirror. It's over, she thought. It's time for me to leave.

When she went out to the patio Andres took her arm and led her to the car. "I don't want to go all the way into Guadalajara," he said. "There's a place only a few miles from here. I'll call the house when we get there and give Nurse Sanchez the number."

"Your mother was better today, Andres. She ate all of her lunch and most of her dinner. I think she looks better too, don't you?"

"I'm not sure." He glanced at Sarah. "I haven't told you how much I appreciate your being here. I hope you haven't jeopardized your job."

"The job's all right. I may not be able to take a vacation for the next ten years but I'm not going to be fired." She stared straight ahead of her. So I was right, she thought. Andres is trying to tell me that I can leave. Leave El Camichín and Richard and... Sarah closed her eyes.

She sat quietly beside him, pale hands folded in her lap. The faint scent of her perfume, one that hinted of silk and lace and soft womanly promises, drifted on the air. Andres longed to touch her but knew that if he did he'd be lost in her softness, in the pale hands that touched him as no other woman ever had.

He couldn't have managed without her these last few days since his mother had been ill. Sarah read aloud when his mother asked her to, or sat quietly beside the bed when Teresa wanted to rest. She'd taken Silvia under her wing, had comforted her and tried to allay her fears. She'd hugged her and comforted her. He knew without asking that Silvia adored her.

It seemed strange to Andres that this quiet woman whom he'd thought of as being weak and vulnerable had become the strength that held them all together through this crisis. The servants turned to her for their instructions. Even Nurse Sanchez relied on her.

The restaurant where Andres stopped had an adjoining bar, and this is where he took Sarah. He found a secluded table and when they were seated ordered a glass of wine for her and a brandy for himself. He waited until the drinks were served before he said, "I needed to talk to you without interruption. I couldn't do that at the house."

Sarah looked at him, waiting. Finally, because she wanted to delay the words that would tell her she was free to leave El Camichín, she said, "Is it your mother? Is there something you haven't told me?"

Andres covered her hand. "No, Sarah. This has nothing to do with Mother. It has to do with us."

So I was right, she thought. He's brought me here to say goodbye.

"I'm grateful that you wanted to stay until Mother was better," Andres said, "and for all the care you've given her."

"Your mother's an unusual woman. She's never condemned or blamed me for what happened with Carlos. She's taken Richard into her home and I'll always love her for that." Sarah took a sip of her wine. "My parents never accepted him, but Doña Teresa did. She has a big heart, Andres, perhaps that's why it's so tired."

"So do you, Sarah."

She looked at him, amazement showing in her eyes. But before she could speak Andres said, "I've been unkind to you. I've said things I'm sorry for and I apologize."

She toyed with the stem of her glass. This is his farewell speech, she thought. She wanted to stop him, to say, Please, it's over. Don't say anything more. Instead she sat there quietly, rolling the stem of her glass back and forth between her fingers.

"I know how hard it's been for you to let Richard go. You didn't try to influence his decision and I respect you for that. We've all come to depend on you, Sarah. You've become a part of our family and we..." Andres took a deep breath. "We...I don't want you to leave. I want you to stay here, at El Camichín."

"Stay?" Sarah's eyes widened in surprise. "I have to support myself, Andres. What would I do here?"

"Marry me."

"A foreigner can't work in Mexico. I..." She stopped. "What did you say?"

"I asked you to marry me, Sarah."

She didn't know whether to laugh or cry, whether to throw herself in his arms or run screaming out of the restaurant.

Andres reached for her hand again. "You don't have to leave, Sarah. Stay here with Richard. You know that would make him happy. And Silvia. She's crazy about you. She—"

"You're asking me to marry you because Silvia likes me?"

"No, dammit, I'm asking you because it's best for everybody. For you and Richard, Mother and Silvia." He finished his brandy and signaled the waitress for another. "You and I..." A muscle jumped in his cheek. "We both know there's a...a strong physical attraction between us."

"And you think that's enough to base a marriage on?"

"It would be more than that, Sarah." He leaned closer. "We'd be a family. You'd be a part of us, just as Richard is. You'd never want for anything, I can promise you that."

Except love, Sarah thought.

"You don't have to give me your answer tonight. I know this has come as a shock and that you need time to think it over."

"Yes," Sarah managed to say. "I need time."

She sipped her wine. They tried not to look at each other. Andres had asked her to marry him. She was too stunned to think beyond that. Never mind that what he had suggested had been more in the nature of an arrangement than a proposal, he'd actually said the words, "Marry me."

But why?

Somewhere in a little corner of Sarah's mind a voice said, What difference does it make? He's offering you a comfortable life. You won't lose Richard if you marry Andres. You love Silvia and Doña Teresa. They're fond of you. Andres has money, you'd never want for anything—except love.

Sarah took a deep breath. Can I live with him day after day? she wondered. Loving him, knowing he doesn't love me?

Andres took her arm when they left the restaurant. But he didn't speak until he turned off the highway leading to El Camichín. When he stopped the car he said, "We could make it work, Sarah."

She leaned back against the seat and closed her eyes, listening to the sound of the cicadas. "You said it would be good for all of us, Andres. For your mother, Richard and Silvia, for me. But what about you? Would it be good for you?"

"I'm forty-one," he said. "There's no one else in my life. It's time I married."

"But why me? Why a gringa like me?"

"You're Richard's mother, you belong here."

"I see."

"Will you think about it?"

"Yes, Andres, I'll think about it."

For a long moment he didn't speak. Then he said, "I'd like you to come to the cabin with me now."

Sarah didn't look at him. "To consummate your... your offer?"

His lips tightened. "I want you," he said.

It was cool inside the cabin. "Would you like anything?" Andres asked as he snapped a light on over his desk. "Coffee? Another glass of wine?"

"Nothing, thank you." Without a word Sarah turned and walked into the bedroom. With her back to him she undressed, turned back the spread, and got into bed.

Andres frowned, puzzled. "If you don't want to..."

"I want to."

He looked at her uncertainly, then quickly stripped off his clothes. When he'd put them over a chair he came to sit on the side of the bed. "We're not romantic children," he said. "We don't have to make declarations of undying love. We both know how good this is between us."

Sarah's heart had never felt so empty.

"If I've offended you by my offer of marriage I'm sorry."

"You haven't offended me."

Andres lifted a strand of her hair. "I'd do my best to make it work, Sarah. There'd never be another woman. I'd never hurt you."

When she didn't respond he lay down beside her. "We both need somebody," he said as he took her hand. "Love is an illusion of the young, Sarah. What we have..." He looked down at her. Then with a sigh he kissed her. "This is what we have, Sarah," he murmured against her lips.

She could feel the beat of his heart against her breast. His body was warm against hers, his hands touched her gently. He kissed her breast and she felt his body tense with need. She didn't want to respond because she wanted to punish him for not loving her. But oh, the touch of his lips against her skin, the touch of his hand on her hip were almost more than she could bear.

He kissed her. "Tell me you want me," he whispered against her lips.

She shook her head as tears stung her eyes, but her lips parted and her arms crept around his shoulders.

"I'll never get enough of you, Sarah. I ache with the need of you. Tell me, Sarah, tell me you want me as much as I want you."

"Yes," she whispered. "Yes, Andres, I want you." She wanted to tell him then that she loved him, that she'd always loved him. Yet not even when her hungry mouth sought his and her body rose to receive him could she find the words.

Love me, her heart cried. Oh, Andres, please love me.

All he said in that final moment of ecstasy was, "It's so good with you, Sarah...so good...so good."

Sarah came to him the next morning when he was saddling his horse. "Do you have a minute?" she asked.

He tightened the cinch under the gelding's belly. "Yes, of course I do."

"I've thought about what you said last night—what you asked me."

"Yes?" he waited.

"I've decided that I will..." She took a deep breath. "I'll marry you, Andres, if that's what you want."

"It's what I want."

"When would you like to have the...the ceremony?"

"Soon. When it's convenient for you."

Convenient... Sarah's hands tightened at her sides.

"Would next week be too soon?"

"No, I guess not." She fought to keep her voice as matter-of-fact as his. "Though we'll need time to tell the family. I don't know how your mother will feel about this."

"She'll approve," he said, too quickly. "I mean...I'm sure she'll be pleased, Sarah. If it's all right with you, we'll tell them tonight."

"Yes, it's all right with me, Andres."

"Good." He started out of the stable with the horse. "Well then, until tonight."

"Yes," she said. "Until tonight. Have a good day, Andres."

Have a good day? My God, she thought, this is insane. How can I go through with it? How can I stand to live like this year after year. He'll say, "Is it convenient if we make love tonight?" And I'll say, "Yes indeed. Have a nice day!"

Sarah wanted to laugh, she wanted to cry. She wanted to run as far away from El Camichín as she could get; at least as far as the meadow.

Without conscious thought she started across the field. Halfway across she began to run. She ran and ran and ran and only when her breath came in gasps and her side hurt so badly that she had to double over in pain, did she stop. She threw herself down on the meadow grass and lay, panting, fighting for breath. Close by she heard the song of a lark, so pure and clear and sweet that she felt tears sting her eyes.

For a long time Sarah lay there. A breeze cooled her flushed cheeks, a curious orange butterfly poised on a blade of grass a few inches from her hand. The earth was warm beneath her back.

I'm going to marry Andres Navarro, Sarah thought. I'm going to be Mrs. Andres Navarro. Mrs. Sarah Navarro. I'll stay for as long as I can stand his not loving me. When I can't stand it any more I'll leave him—if he doesn't leave me first.

She didn't know why he had asked her to be his wife. But he *had* asked her and she had said yes.

God help us both, Sarah prayed as she lay there in the sunny meadow. Help us both.

Chapter Sixteen

That night was to be an occasion. Sarah felt she needed armor to protect herself, so she took special pains dressing for dinner. She washed her hair and brushed it until it shone and curled softly around her face. She touched gold eyeshadow on her lids, blush to her cheekbones, coral to her lips. She wore a summer-blue dress.

When she finished dressing she stood in front of the mirror. I'm ready, she thought. Ready to go out and announce to the family that Andres and I are going to be married. Not even in dreams had Sarah envisioned this moment, yet here it was, she was engaged to marry Andres Navarro.

"Wow!" Richard said when Sarah walked into the dining room. "You look like a million bucks, Mom."

"Thank you, darling." She looked at Andres.

He turned to busy himself at the bar. With his back to her he said, "Would you care for a drink?"

"No, thank you."

"I've opened a bottle of champagne. I thought we might have a toast later."

"A toast?" Silvia looked at him inquiringly. "To what, Uncle Andres?"

"You'll find out soon enough. Now suppose the four of us pay a visit to Grandmother before we have dinner. I have some news and I'd like her to hear it."

"What news?" Richard asked. "What's going on?"

Andres put his arm around Richard's shoulders. "You'll have to come along if you want to find out."

As they started down the corridor Richard turned back to raise his eyebrows at Sarah in question and she thought, please let it be all right with him. When he'd been younger Richard hadn't liked anyone she dated. "Why do you want to go out with him?" he'd always said with a scowl, no matter who the "him" might be. As Richard had grown older he hadn't been as vocal in his objections, but he'd been suspicious of every man Sarah went out with. How would he feel now when Andres announced that he and Sarah were going to be married?

"What's going on?" Silvia whispered. "Do you know?"

Sarah nodded as she put her arm through Silvia's. "I hope it's something that will make you happy."

"What in the world . . . ?" Silvia's brown eyes sparkled with excitement. "I know! I bet we're going to welcome Rico officially to the family. That's it, isn't it?"

"You'll know in a few minutes." Sarah squeezed Silvia's hand and felt a sudden, unexpected glow of happiness. It would be fun, she thought, living in the same house with Silvia, watching her grow into young womanhood, sharing her secrets and her dreams. For a moment Sarah almost believed that everything would be all right. She'd have Richard. Doña Teresa was fond of her. Andres . . .

His back was to her, his arm still around Richard. He looked larger than life, she thought, every inch a man. The powerful, dominant male, master of the family, head of the house of Navarro.

He too had dressed for the occasion in tailored dark gray trousers and a white linen *guayabera*. His face was as solemn as Sarah's tonight and she wondered, seeing his profile as he turned to open his mother's bedroom door, if he shared her fear and uncertainty.

Once more she thought, why did he ask me to marry him?

"Good evening, Mother. Do you feel like visitors?" Andres glanced at Nurse Sanchez. "Why don't you have your dinner?" he said. "We'll be here for a while."

"Of course, sir. Thank you."

"Well?" Teresa said when the nurse left. "What's this all about?"

"We don't know, Grandmother," Silvia said. "*Tío* won't tell us."

"Perhaps he'll tell me." Teresa looked from her son to Sarah.

"Sarah and I are going to be married, Mother," Andres said in a formal voice. "We'd like your blessing."

"Married!" Richard stared openmouthed at his mother. "Married?"

Before Sarah could respond Teresa reached for her hand. "My dear," she said. "My dear Sarah. Come, sit here. You too, Andres, on the other side." She clasped their hands in hers. "What wonderful news. You've made me happier than I can ever tell you. Of course you have my blessing." She brought their hands together across the bed.

For the first time that evening Andres really looked at Sarah. In the light of the bedside lamp her eyes looked luminous. She's beautiful, he thought with a touch of amazement. He looked down at the pale hand clasped in his. Her fingers were slender, her rounded nails were polished. In wonder he rubbed his thumb across the back of her hand and felt the fragility of her bones. His eyes met hers and he felt, he felt . . .

"I can't believe it!" Silvia cried. Then she was on the bed too, hugging Sarah, hugging Andres, hugging her grandmother. "Oh, isn't this the most exciting thing that ever happened? Can I be your bridesmaid, Sarah? When's the wedding?''

"Mom?" Richard touched Sarah's shoulder. "Con...congratulations." His eyes were wide with shock. Then suddenly he grinned. "Hey," he said. "This means you're going to stay here, doesn't it? You won't have to leave." He tried to get past Silvia so that he too could hug his mother.

Sarah put both arms around him. "Is it all right?" she whispered.

"All right? It's terrific!"

"What about me?" Andres stood up and when Richard came around the bed to shake his hand Andres gave him a hearty Mexican *abrazo*.

When the excitement settled down a bit, they all sat close to Teresa. "Tell me about it," she said. "When will the wedding take place?"

"We thought next week, Mother. You should be feeling better by then."

"By then? I'm feeling better right now. But I can't plan a wedding in a week, Andres. There are people to invite. Sarah's parents and her friends who might want to come from the United States."

"We thought we'd have a small wedding." Andres looked uncomfortable. "Just the family."

"Nonsense." Teresa's voice was firm. To Sarah she said, "You must invite your family, my dear, and as many of your friends you think can come. This is your wedding, too." And as though that had been settled she said, "Now about the engagement party."

"An engagement party? That's out of the question," Andres said. "You're not well enough—"

"I will be. Sarah and Silvia can make all the arrangements about the food and music. It's too late to send out invitations but I can telephone our friends. Let's see, this is Tuesday. If we have the engagement party a week from tomorrow we could have the wedding the following Sunday." Teresa smiled at Sarah. "That should give you time enough to get your family and friends here, shouldn't it, dear?"

"Yes, but..." Sarah looked at Andres. "I think Andres would rather—"

"Men don't know about these things, Sarah, they leave it up to women." Doña Teresa leaned back against the pillows and smiled. "It's all settled."

"Mother, I—" Andres tried to say.

But Doña Teresa held up her hand. "I'm tired now. I have to rest."

"But, Mother, I—"

Doña Teresa closed her eyes. The matter had been settled.

"I think big weddings are fun," Silvia said when she sat down to dinner. "What'll we wear, Sarah? Can we go to Guadalajara tomorrow? I know a darling little boutique that has absolutely gorgeous clothes. How are you going to wear your hair? Can I have mine cut like Sarah's, Uncle Andres?"

"No, you can't." He frowned at her. He frowned at Sarah. "I didn't plan on all this fuss," he said.

"Yeah, but you know women, *Tío* Andres." Richard sighed. "You gotta give them their way about some things, and weddings are one of them, I guess." He looked at the bottle of champagne cooling beside Andres's chair. "Are we going to have a toast now?"

"It seems appropriate." Andres poured champagne into four crystal goblets. He filled two of the glasses to the brim. The two that he filled only halfway he handed to Silvia and Richard. Then he gave one of the goblets to Sarah and for the second time that evening his eyes met hers.

"To Mom and Andres," Richard said. "Bottoms up."

"Richard!" Silvia said as Sarah burst into laughter. "That's the most unromantic toast I've ever heard."

"Then you say something."

"I don't know any toasts."

"Well say something!"

Silvia looked at Sarah. "Would a poem be all right?" she asked.

"A poem would be fine," Sarah said with a smile.

"Okay." Silvia cleared her throat. Then she raised her glass and recited:

"Come live with me and be my love,
And we will all the pleasures prove,
That valleys, groves, or hills, or fields,
Or woods and steepy mountains yields."

"That's by Christopher Marlowe," Silvia said. "It's called 'The Passionate Shepherd to His Love'." She blushed. "So let's drink to Sarah and Uncle Andres."

"That was lovely, Silvia, thank you." Sarah looked across the table at Andres.

"I'm not sure I approve of you reading poems about passionate shepherds, Silvia, but the words were very nice. Thank you." Andres raised his glass and touched it to Sarah's and thought again how beautiful she was. He liked her in blue. She'd been wearing blue the first time he'd seen her. When they were married he'd ask her to buy only blue dresses. Then he remembered how she looked in apricot, and in ivory, and knew that she was beautiful, no matter what she wore.

I'm falling in love with her, he thought with a shock. His hand froze in midair, the breath caught in his throat. My God, I love her.

He watched the play of candlelight on her face, the way her hair curled around her face, the curve of her slender fingers against the stem of the crystal goblet. Soon this lovely woman would be his wife. What would it be like, he wondered, to lie beside Sarah in the darkness and know that she would be there when he awoke? What would it be like to see her face each morning? Gently to kiss her awake?

I love her, Andres thought again, almost gasping aloud with the wonder of it. He wanted to take her hand across the table and say, I love you, Sarah.

1. How do you rate _____
   (Please print book TITLE)

   1.6 ☐ excellent   .4 ☐ good   .2 ☐ not so good
    .5 ☐ very good   .3 ☐ fair   .1 ☐ poor

   HABCD

2. How likely are you to purchase another book:
   in this *series*?   by this *author*?
   2.1 ☐ definitely would purchase   3.1 ☐ definitely would purchase
    .2 ☐ probably would puchase   .2 ☐ probably would puchase
    .3 ☐ probably would not purchase   .3 ☐ probably would not purchase
    .4 ☐ definitely would not purchase   .4 ☐ definitely would not purchase

3. How does this book compare with similar books you usually read?
   4.1 ☐ far better than others   .2 ☐ better than others   .3 ☐ about the
    .4 ☐ not as good   .5 ☐ definitely not as good   same

4. Please check the statements you feel best describe this book.

   5. ☐ Easy to read   6. ☐ Too much violence/anger
   7. ☐ Realistic conflict   8. ☐ Wholesome/not too sexy
   9. ☐ Too sexy   10. ☐ Interesting characters
   11. ☐ Original plot   12. ☐ Especially romantic
   13. ☐ Not enough humor   14. ☐ Difficult to read
   15. ☐ Didn't like the subject   16. ☐ Good humor in story
   17. ☐ Too predictable   18. ☐ Not enough description of setting
   19. ☐ Believable characters   20. ☐ Fast paced
   21. ☐ Couldn't put the book down   22. ☐ Heroine too juvenile/weak/silly
   23. ☐ Made me feel good   24. ☐ Too many foreign/unfamiliar words
   25. ☐ Hero too dominating   26. ☐ Too wholesome/not sexy enough
   27. ☐ Not enough romance   28. ☐ Liked the setting
   29. ☐ Ideal hero   30. ☐ Heroine too independent
   31. ☐ Slow moving   32. ☐ Unrealistic conflict
   33. ☐ Not enough suspense   34. ☐ Sensuous/not too sexy
   35. ☐ Liked the subject   36. ☐ Too much description of setting

5. What *most* prompted you to buy this book?
   37. ☐ Read others in series   38. ☐ Title   39. ☐ Cover art
   40. ☐ Friend's recommendation   41. ☐ Author   42. ☐ In-store display
   43. ☐ TV, radio or magazine ad   44. ☐ Price   45. ☐ Story outline
   46. ☐ Ad inside other books   47. ☐ Other _____ (please specify)

6. Please indicate how many romance paperbacks you read in a month.
   48.1 ☐ 1 to 4   .2 ☐ 5 to 10   .3 ☐ 11 to 15   .4 ☐ more than 15

7. Please indicate your sex and age group.
   49.1 ☐ Male   50.1 ☐ under 15   .3 ☐ 25-34   .5 ☐ 50-64
    .2 ☐ Female   .2 ☐ 15-24   .4 ☐ 35-49   .6 ☐ 65 or older

8. Have you any additional comments about this book?
   _____ (51)
   _____ (53)

Thank you for completing and returning this questionnaire.

NAME
(Please Print)

ADDRESS

CITY

ZIP CODE

BUSINESS REPLY MAIL

FIRST CLASS   PERMIT NO. 717   BUFFALO, NY

POSTAGE WILL BE PAID BY ADDRESSEE

NATIONAL READER SURVEYS

901 Fuhrmann Blvd.
P.O. Box 1395
Buffalo, N.Y. 14240-9961

But what if she said, Love? That wasn't part of the bargain, Andres. You've already asked too much of me. Don't ask that.

He wished that she loved him. He wished that she had said yes to his proposal of marriage because of love, because she wanted to be with him. He'd told himself that he was doing this for his mother but he knew now that it wasn't true. It never had been true.

Andres tightened his hand around the stem of the goblet. You've been a fool, he told himself. You've been jealous of a dead man, of something that happened fifteen years ago. But it's not too late, he thought. Sarah's going to marry me. I still have a chance to make her love me, and when she does I'll tell her that I love her. Afterward, when we're married.

He raised his glass and touching it to Sarah's again said, "To beauty."

"Thank you." She looked surprised. Her eyes met his over the rim of her glass and her breath caught in her throat. There was an expression on Andres's face that she'd never seen before. His eyes, cave-black and intense, questioned, even as they challenged, implored, even as they demanded. She was entrapped, lost in the compelling darkness of his gaze, not aware that her hand trembled.

"Why couldn't you have said something like that?" Silvia said to Richard. "To beauty. That's very nice, *Tío*."

Sarah put the glass down without having sipped from it. For a moment she'd almost thought she'd seen a look of love.

When the meal ended the two young people went to the *sala* to watch television. "Let's get some air," Andres said as he pulled out Sarah's chair, and taking her hand led her to the patio. She chose a lounge near the gardenia bushes, picked one of the white flowers, and idly brushed it against her lips.

"Well, we've told them," Andres said. "I think everyone was pleased."

"I worried about Richard's reaction. He's never liked any of the men I went out with."

"Were there a lot of them?"

"Not many." Sarah twisted the gardenia between her fingers.

"No serious relationships?"

"One or two semiserious."

"Why didn't you ever marry?"

"I don't know, Andres. It just never seemed right."

"And this is?"

"I don't know."

He moved so that he could sit next to her. "I'm curious, Sarah. Why did you agree to marry me?"

"Why did you ask me?"

Andres looked at her. He took the gardenia out of her hand and brought her fingers to his lips. The scent of the flower was still on them. He closed his eyes and ran his tongue over her fingertips. Every time I touch her, he thought, I want her. He opened his eyes and pulled her into his arms. "Sarah," he whispered against her lips. "Oh, Sarah."

He heard her startled gasp, felt her tremble against him, and thought his body would explode with need.

"Come to the cabin with me," he said. "I want to be alone with you."

Sarah stiffened in his arms. "Richard and Silvia," she said, "they—"

"They're watching television, they'll never miss us."

Sarah shook her head.

"Then we'll wait until they're in bed."

"No, Andres." Sarah sat up and swung her legs off the chaise. "I'm sorry but I'd rather not. I know this will sound strange to you but I'd like us to wait until we're married."

"But we've already made love, Sarah. Why is tonight any different?"

"I'm not sure. Maybe it's because now it's official. The family is involved, there's going to be an engagement party and a wedding and I'd...I'd like to wait until then. Does that make any sense?"

"No!" Andres got up. He glared at her. But as he looked at her his face softened and he said, "Yes, I guess it does." He smoothed one of the curls on the side of her face. "You go in now. I'm going to stay out here for a while."

Sarah looked at him, puzzled. "All right, Andres," she said. "Good night."

As Andres watched her go he felt his desire ebb into something that was a strange new feeling. He understood how Sarah felt, he even approved of it. Twelve days from now, he thought. I can wait that long because I've already waited a lifetime.

He picked up the gardenia that she'd left on the chaise. Its petals felt soft against his fingers, as soft as Sarah's skin. He brought it to his face and rubbed his lips against it. Sarah, he thought, my love.

Chapter Seventeen

That's just about the best-looking man I've ever seen," Aunt Jo said when Andres excused himself to go to the bar. "I can't imagine why someone hasn't nabbed him before this. Talk about tall, dark and handsome! He gives a whole new meaning to the word macho." She grinned at Sarah. "He's going to be a handful, kiddo. I hope you've got the stamina to keep up with him."

"I'll do my best," Sarah said with a smile. "I'm so glad you're here, Aunt Jo. It's wonderful to see you again."

"You too, Sarah. I'm sorry your mother and father couldn't make it. Millie said they were..." Jo looked embarrassed. "It was something about your dad's work I think. He couldn't get away right now."

"I understand." Sarah had phoned her parents the day after she and Andres announced their plans to the family.

"Navarro?" her mother had said. "You're going to marry Andres Navarro? The brother of the man who...?" Her gasp was audible. "Really," she said. "Sarah, really!"

"I'd like you and Dad to come to the wedding, Mother. It's going to be a week from Sunday."

"I don't think your father will... I'm sure it's impossible, Sarah. His business..." She didn't finish the sentence.

"If it's a question of money, Mother, I'll send you a check for the airfare. You and Dad could stay here at the ranch. There's plenty of room."

"It's not the money. We couldn't stay at the ranch. I wouldn't be comfortable there, knowing that's where you..." Millie Maxwell cleared her throat. "I hope you know what you're doing, Sarah. I can't imagine that you want your son raised among those... those people. But that's your business, I suppose. Your father and I have always wanted what was best for you and..."

Sarah had closed her eyes and tried not to listen as her mother's voice droned on.

When she phoned her aunt, Jo had squealed with delight. "I'll be on the first plane out of Miami," she said. And here she was, looking as beautiful and as chic as ever, salt-and-pepper hair cut in the latest style, dressed in tailored slacks and a bright orange cotton sweater.

"I understand why my folks aren't coming," Sarah said. "It's all right, I'm not unhappy about it."

"What about Ellie? Did you phone her?"

Sarah nodded. "She'll be here on Thursday, in time for the party."

"Is she going to be your maid of honor?"

"No, Silvia wanted to be and I couldn't refuse her."

"Of course not." Jo's eyes searched Sarah's. "It's working out for you, isn't it, Sarah? You've finally found what you've been looking for."

"I don't think I was looking, but yes, Aunt Jo, I guess I have. Richard loves it here. His grandmother's crazy about him and so is Silvia. Andres is teaching him all about the ranch. He mends fences and ropes cows, works hard and loves every minute of it. I know he's going to be happy."

"So much for Richard." Jo looked at her inquiringly. "What about you? You're the one who's getting married and all I'm hearing about is Richard. Is anything wrong?"

"No, of course not." She flushed. "It's just that—"

But at that moment Andres returned carrying a tray with three frosty margaritas. He handed one to Jo, then gave Sarah hers and said, *"Salud."*

"Cheers." Jo smiled at him over the rim of her glass. "Thanks for letting me arrive so early, Andres.

The invitation was to the wedding, and that's still a week away. But when Sarah told me she was getting married I'm afraid I couldn't wait to see her."

"We're delighted you're here. And if Sarah hasn't already invited you for Christmas I want to invite you now."

"Thank you, Andres. Invitation accepted. I can't think of any place I'd rather be than here with the two of you." She turned to Sarah. "Where are the two of you going on your honeymoon?"

"I don't think we'll be able to get away," Sarah said. "Doña Teresa isn't well; we wouldn't want to leave her."

"We can manage a few days in Acapulco," Andres said. "I've already spoken to Nurse Sanchez and she's agreed to stay on until we return. When Mother's better we'll take a longer trip, to Europe if that's what Sarah would like to do."

Jo beamed as she reached for Sarah's hand. "I'm so happy for the two of you. You've got it all, Sarah, this beautiful place, two great kids, and love."

And love, Sarah thought. She didn't look at Andres.

The following day Sarah, Jo, and Silvia drove into Guadalajara to Silvia's "darling little boutique." Sarah tried on half a dozen dresses before she narrowed down her choice to a floor-length lavender wool jersey and a short, but elegant blue Charmeuse.

"Get the blue," Silvia said decisively. "Uncle Andres likes you in blue."

"And how do you know that, Señorita Navarro?" Sarah asked with a smile as she turned in front of the mirror.

"I've seen the way he looks at you when you're wearing it. Like the night the two of you told us you were going to get married. Uncle Andres couldn't keep his eyes off you all through dinner."

Sarah felt hot color flush her cheeks, remembering that as soon as dinner finished Andres had wanted her to go to the cabin with him. That wasn't love, she wanted to tell Sylvia, that was plain old-fashioned lust. That's what I've agreed to settle for. But bought the blue dress nonetheless.

"That does it," she said. "I'm starving. Let's go to lunch."

"What about your negligee?" Jo asked.

"I . . . I have enough lingerie."

"Sarah!" Aunt Jo looked shocked. "You have to have something new for your honeymoon! Now come on, pick something out and I'll buy it for you."

But it was Jo and Silvia who did the picking. Silvia's choice was a black lace teddy. Aunt Jo looked at it, trying not to giggle, and said, "I don't think so, kiddo." She lifted an ivory satin and alençon lace off the quilted hanger, held it and the matching robe up to Sarah and said, "This is perfect, Sarah. Go try it on."

The satin slithered over her body. She looked at herself in the mirror and knew that Aunt Jo had been right, the gown was perfect. It molded the curves of

her body, it made her skin look rosy-pink. If only...
She felt a pang of sadness...if only...

"What kind of a ring have you decided on?" Aunt
Jo asked over lunch.

"A plain wedding band I imagine," Sarah said.
"We haven't discussed it. Andres has been awfully
busy with the ranch. He hasn't said anything about a
ring yet."

"Then you say something," Aunt Jo said indig-
nantly.

"No, a ring really isn't that important." Certainly
not to Andres, Sarah thought, that's why he hasn't
said anything. The wedding is only a formality, a necessary part of our arrangement.

"You have to have a ring," Jo said.

"All right, all right. I'll tell him to get a plain gold
band—just to make you happy."

That night as Sarah was dressing for dinner, Andres knocked on the French doors of her bedroom and
when she opened them he said, "May I come in? I
have something for you."

"Yes, of course." Sarah looked at him curiously.

Andres handed her a small velvet box. "I hope these
are all right, Sarah. I had to guess your size. If they're
not right, or if you'd rather have something else, we
can return them."

Sarah looked up at him. Then she opened the box.
A star sapphire, surrounded by a circle of diamonds,
winked up at her. The wedding ring next to it was set
in a tailored row of diamonds and smaller sapphires.

"They're . . . they're beautiful," Sarah said.

"If you'd rather have a diamond solitaire—"

"No, no, I love the sapphire, Andres. Thank you."

"Try it on, Sarah. The jeweler promised to fix it right away if it didn't fit." He took the ring out of the box and when Sarah held out her left hand he slipped it on her finger.

"It's perfect." Tears misted her eyes as she looked up at him.

"Sarah?"

Time stood still as they looked into each other's eyes. Andres put his hands on her shoulders and drew her closer. "Sarah," he said again, and kissed her.

Andres had never kissed her like this. He had never held her so tenderly or whispered her name so gently against her lips. "It's going to be all right, Sarah," he said. "We'll make it be all right."

"Yes, Andres." For the first time since he had asked her to marry him, Sarah felt a surge of hope that perhaps, after all, Andres would learn to love her. When he did she would tell him how she felt, how she'd always felt. She could wait now because she had hope that some day, God willing, Andres would love her as she loved him.

Ellie arrived on Thursday afternoon before the engagement party. "I told John and the boys they'd have to fend for themselves," she told Sarah. "I wouldn't miss your wedding for anything in the world. It's great that your aunt is here. Too bad your parents couldn't make it."

"It was their choice not to come," Sarah said. "And you know what, Ellie? I'm damned if I'm going to lose any sleep over it."

"Good for you." Ellie opened her suitcase and held up a dress. "Will this do for the party tonight?"

"It's beautiful."

"What are you wearing?"

"A Mexican-style dress, white cotton with lots of embroidery." Sarah took Ellie's hand. "It's great to have you here, friend. It's like old times."

"Better than old times." Ellie hugged her. "I'm so happy for you, Sarah, so glad that everything's worked out." She hesitated. "Does Andres know about Richard?"

Sarah nodded. "Everyone knows, Ellie, and they've been wonderful."

"That's great," Ellie said. "Be happy, pal."

I am happy, Sarah thought. I didn't expect to be but I am. From the patio she could hear the music of the mariachis and the voices of arriving guests. Tonight she'd meet friends of the Navarros, and on Sunday afternoon these same people would be guests at her wedding.

She and Andres hadn't been alone since the night he'd given her the ring. He'd been busy on the ranch during the day and in the evening the family was always present. Sarah smiled at herself in the mirror as she dressed. Even though she hadn't been alone with

Andres it seemed to her that in a strange way they'd grown closer. There was something in the way he spoke, and in the way he looked at her. It made her think that perhaps Andres wasn't marrying her because of Richard or Silvia or because he was forty-one. He just might have asked her to marry him because he cared.

She was still smiling when one of the maids knocked on the door and handed her a tissue-wrapped gardenia. "I was told to give this to you," the maid said.

"Gracias." Sarah held the gardenia to her face for a moment. He does care about me, she thought. He does care.

Her face radiated happiness when she stepped out onto the patio to stand between Andres and Doña Teresa in an informal receiving line.

Introductions were made, congratulations were offered. Sarah shook hands with people whose names she forgot two minutes later. The women scrutinized her, the men kissed her hand and told Andres how lucky he was. When at last the line dwindled, Andres led his mother to a chair and when she was comfortably settled with friends he said to Sarah, "Now I'd like to dance with my bride to be."

She had no idea what miracle had brought this change in Andres, but she thanked heaven for it. When he put his arms around her she said, "Thank you for the gardenia, Andres."

"You're welcome." He smiled down at her. "Have I told you you look especially lovely tonight, Señorita Maxwell."

"Thank you, Señor Navarro."

"I wonder if you're free on Sunday afternoon."

"I'm afraid not, Señor Navarro. I have a date to be married on Sunday."

"Really? Who's the fortunate man?"

"Oh, I don't think you know him. He's handsome and charming and—"

"Rich?"

"Of course." She smiled. "That's why I'm marrying him."

The hand against her back pressed her closer. "You're wicked," he murmured as he nipped her earlobe.

It was a wonderful evening. The patio glowed with colored lights, the mariachi music was lively, the wine was delicious. As Sarah whirled around the floor in Andres's arms she thought, I wish this evening could last forever. She knew she'd never been happier.

A little before midnight tables were set up around the fountain and the maids served a light dinner of seafood crepes and fresh fruit salad, along with chilled champagne. Toasts were drunk, good wishes were offered.

"It's a wonderful party," Ellie told Sarah. "And isn't it great that Richard's so at home here?" She squeezed Sarah's hand. "It's all worked out, hasn't it,

Sarah? You really are going to live happily ever after."

"Yes," Sarah said, "I think I am." She smiled across the table at Andres. He raised his glass to hers and their fingers touched. This is the happiest night of my life, Sarah thought. It's a new beginning, the beginning of my life with Andres.

After they had eaten he turned to his mother. "It's late, *madre*," he said. "I think you should rest now."

"Yes, perhaps I should. If you and Sarah don't mind perhaps the two of you could see me to my room."

Teresa said good-night to her guests. "Please don't feel that because I must retire you have to leave. The mariachis will be here for another hour at least. Enjoy yourselves. And thank you for coming. I'll see all of you on Sunday." Then, with Sarah on one side of her and Andres on the other, she went down the corridor to her room.

When they went inside Sarah said, "Would you like me to help you undress?"

"No, dear, you and Andres go back to our guests. One of the maids will be in soon." She kissed Sarah's cheek, then Andres's. "You've made me happier than you can ever know," she said. "When I first suggested to Andres that he ask you to marry him he was reluctant, but now..."

The words hung in the air as Doña Teresa's eyes widened in horror. She looked at Andres, then at Sarah's stricken face.

"I . . . I didn't mean . . ." she gasped. "I . . ." With a cry of pain she sank to the bed and covered her face with her hands.

Sarah felt frozen. It was as though she'd been struck a blow that had rendered her dumb. She looked at the other woman's bowed head, then gazed at Andres and saw from the shock and the shame on his face that Doña Teresa had spoken the truth.

Suddenly everything was painfully clear. Doña Teresa had been ill. She'd asked this of Andres and he'd given in to her. That's why he'd been so cold when he asked Sarah to marry him. That's why now, in front of his mother and their guests, he'd pretended to care for her. Everything . . . everything had been a lie to placate a sick and elderly mother. Sarah looked away from Andres and knew she never wanted to see him again.

She put her hand on Doña Teresa's shoulder. "Don't cry," she said in a dead little voice. "It's all right. I'd better get back to the guests. Andres will stay with you." She didn't look at him.

She went back to the party and said all the right things. When Aunt Jo asked, "What's the matter?" Sarah smiled a terrible fixed smile and said, "Nothing's the matter. Everything's great."

"Sarah . . . ?"

Sarah had already turned away. She danced with all of the men who asked her, she drank champagne, and all the while she smiled her terrible fixed smile.

The hour grew late, the guests dwindled to a few hardy souls. Richard and Silvia said good-night. Aunt Jo and Ellie exchanged worried glances. Andres came back, looking pale as he went to Sarah and said, "May I speak to you alone for a moment?"

"No, you may not." She picked a half-filled bottle of champagne off the bar. "A little nightcap," she said to Ellie. She kissed Jo's cheek and clung for a moment to her aunt. When she let her go she stepped back and bumped against one of the tables.

"Let me help you." Andres put out a hand to steady her.

Sarah looked at him then. "Don't touch me," she said. "Don't ever touch me again."

She heard Aunt Jo's gasp and Ellie's startled, "Sarah!" Then she broke away and before anyone could stop her ran down the long empty corridor to her room.

Chapter Eighteen

"Where is she?" Andres demanded.

Jo looked at him, her face just as angry as his. "What possible difference could it make to you?" she asked in a scathing tone.

"What difference? I'm going to marry her in two days."

"I think not."

Andres stared at her. "What in the hell are you talking about? Where is Sarah?"

"I won't tell you, Andres." Jo faced him, hands on her hips. "I can't believe that this family has managed to hurt Sarah a second time," she said. "Just as soon as I can I'm going to take her away from here and

I'm going to do my damnedest to see that none of you ever hurt her again.''

"You don't know what you're talking about, Mrs. Kelsey.''

"Don't I? I know what she suffered before, Andres, because I was there. You weren't and neither was your brother. Sarah came to me because her parents didn't want her in Chicago. She almost died when Richard was born, did you know that? The doctor was so sure she was going to he made me send for her parents. But that was a waste of time because they didn't bother to come.''

Andres's face was white. "Please tell me where she is,'' he said.

"No.'' Jo touched the note in her pocket.

She'd known last night that something was terribly wrong. When the house was quiet she'd gone to Sarah's room. There was no answer when she knocked. "Please,'' she said. "Please, Sarah, let me in.''

Sarah had finally opened the door; her face had been ravaged with tears. And she'd told Jo, told her that Andres had asked her to marry him only because of his mother. He didn't love her, he didn't even like her very much. Everything had been a sham. "I can't talk about it now,'' Sarah had said. "Maybe in the morning.''

In the morning she'd been gone, leaving a note that said, "Please tell Ellie I'm sorry I dragged her all the way here. Tell Richard I'll phone him. If you need to reach me I'll be at the Villa Monte Alegre on Lake

Chapala. Please don't tell anyone. I hope you'll stay at the ranch until I return; it will help Richard if you do, and we can go back to Miami together."

Now Jo Kelsey looked at Andres with cold, uncompromising eyes. "No," she said again. "I won't tell you where Sarah is."

"Mrs. Kelsey, Jo, please..." He ran a tired hand across his unshaven face. As long as he lived he'd never forget the expression on Sarah's face when his mother had said, "I suggested to Andres that he ask you to marry him."

He had to find her. He had to tell her how sorry he was that it had taken him such a long time to know that he loved her.

He looked at Jo Kelsey. "Can we sit down?" he said. "I'd like to talk to you." He took her arm and led her out to the patio. When they were seated he said, "That summer when Sarah first came to us she was the most beautiful young woman I'd ever seen. And it scared the hell out of me because of Carlos. He was twenty, Jo. He was a good-looking boy. By the time he was seventeen he'd bedded half the girls within a fifty-mile radius of El Camichín." Andres hesitated. "Maybe that was partly our fault, the family's fault I mean."

Joe looked at him. "I don't understand."

"We'd already decided Carlos's future for him. He was going to marry Maria Escobar because our families had been friends for years and because a part of the Escobar land would come with the marriage."

"But this is the twentieth century. Marriages aren't arranged today."

"Aren't they?" Andres's smile was ironic. "This wasn't a you'll-marry-or-else decree, it was simply understood that when Carlos turned twenty-one he and Maria would marry." He looked at Jo, then away. "Carlos wanted one last fling before he settled down."

"And Sarah was the fling?"

Andres nodded. "I took one look at her and knew I didn't want Carlos anywhere near her. I tried to tell myself she was an experienced little gringa who knew her way around, that she was bad for Carlos." Andres shook his head. "Bad for Carlos! Once he made up his mind to have her, Sarah didn't stand a chance."

He got up and began to pace back and forth. "I tried to keep an eye on them. When I was afraid things might be getting out of control I told Sarah about Carlos's engagement to Maria. She looked so shocked, so devastated, that I put my arms around her. I kissed her." Andres took a deep breath. "I've remembered that kiss for fifteen years, Jo. When I saw Sarah again it was as though time had stood still. I think I've loved her for fifteen years."

"But if you loved her—"

"I didn't tell her how I felt, Jo. When I found out about Richard—when I learned that he was Carlos's son—I told myself there could never be anything between us." His face was bitter with self-recrimination. "Carlos had had her; I didn't want her."

Jo started to get up but Andres put a restraining hand on her arm. "I acted like a self-righteous, sanctimonious fool. I know that now. I want a chance to make it up to her, to show her how much I care."

He stood up and looking down at Jo Kelsey said, "When Mother was so ill, when we thought we were going to lose her..." He took a deep shaking breath before he said, "Mother's fond of Sarah. She thought Sarah's place was here at El Camichín with Richard. She asked me to marry Sarah, to keep her here."

"So you asked her to marry you because your *mother* wanted you to?" Jo's voice was disdainful. "My God, Andres, how could you possibly have thought a marriage like that would work?"

"I didn't think, I only knew that I wanted Sarah. But something happened to me, Jo, the night we announced our engagement. I looked at Sarah across the table and suddenly I knew that I had always loved her. I didn't expect her to love me, not after all I've put her through, but I thought that in time we could work it out." He looked at Jo. "I've got to find her," he said. "Sarah has to know that I love her. That I value her."

For a long time neither of them spoke. Finally Jo reached in her pocket for Sarah's note and handed it to Andres. She touched his hand and in a voice choked with tears said, "Well, go ahead. What are you waiting for?"

Sarah watched the fishermen bring in their evening catch. Thunderheads rolled in low over the lake as they folded their nets and secured their boats against the coming storm. When the first spatters of rain dampened the sand, tourists headed for their cars or down the beach to their hotels. But still Sarah stood, looking out over the white-capped water, watching the gulls, listening to their cries as they dived for discarded fish. It was a sharp sound, a lonely sound.

Finally, when the rain began to come down in torrents, Sarah, head bent against the rising wind, went back to her hotel. After she had showered she wrapped herself in a large white towel and dried her hair, then she put on her bathrobe and went to the sitting room window to watch the rain.

She had left El Camichín at dawn in Ellie's rental car, leaving a note telling Aunt Jo where she would be. What she had done hadn't been fair to the others, especially to Ellie and Aunt Jo after they'd traveled a couple of thousand miles to see her. Tomorrow... she couldn't think about tomorrow yet.

Sarah sat for a long time, chin on her drawn-up knees, watching the rain. Sooner or later she'd have to go back, if only to pack her clothes and explain to Richard why she had to leave him. He could come to visit her in Miami, but she would never again return to El Camichín.

When a knock on the door sounded she said, "Who is it?" and a maid answered, "It is I, señorita."

"Just a moment." Sarah brushed her hair back off her face and opened the door. The chambermaid handed her a tissue-wrapped gardenia. "A man asked me to give this to you," she said with a smile.

Sarah touched the cool white petals of the flower. "I don't want it," she said in a faint voice. Then looking up she saw Andres coming down the corridor toward her and quickly stepped back and closed the door.

"Sarah! I want to talk to you."

She leaned her back against the door. "Go away," she said, "I don't want to see you."

"Sarah, please. Open the door." He rattled the knob then pounded on the door with his fist.

"Please, señor," the maid said. "If you continue with this I will be forced to call the manager."

"Then call him. I'm not leaving until I see Señora Carlson."

"All *right*!" Sarah threw the door open. Hands on her hips she faced Andres. "Come in if you insist, but believe me, we have nothing to talk about." She turned away and went to stand by the window, looking out at the slanting rain, shoulders stiffening when she heard the door close. With her back to him she said, "How did you talk Aunt Jo into telling you where I was?"

"I told her that I loved you and that I'd been a damn fool." Andres crossed the room. He put his hands on Sarah's shoulders and said, "Come home with me. Come back to El Camichín."

Sarah pulled away and facing him said, "Why should I? You only asked me to marry you because your mother wanted you to. You don't love me, Andres."

"Of course I love you. I've loved you since the day we stood on the hill looking down on El Camichín." He touched a strand of her still damp hair. "When you came back it was like having a second chance, Sarah, and I began to fall in love with you all over again. Then I found out about Richard . . . about Carlos . . . and something happened to me, to the way I felt, the way I thought."

"I know what you thought, Andres." Tears of anger filled Sarah's eyes. "And I know how you felt every time you made love to me. I didn't live up to your idea of what the perfect woman should be, did I?"

"I was wrong and I'm sorry. But I love you, Sarah." His eyes darkened with intensity. "I tried to tell myself that I didn't love you, that I'd only asked you to marry me because of my mother. But that isn't true. The night that we announced our engagement I looked across the table at you and I thought you were the most beautiful woman I'd ever seen." He took her hand and brought it to his lips. "But it wasn't just your beauty I saw, my darling, it was everything about you. I wanted to tell you then, in front of Richard and Silvia, but I didn't because I thought you didn't love me, that you couldn't love me after the way I'd acted."

Andres stepped closer. "I can't lose you again, Sarah. Please, give me another chance to make you love me."

She looked into his cave-black eyes. She saw the fear there, and the love. With a trembling hand she touched his face. "I've always loved you, Andres," she said.

He took a deep, shaking breath. "Will you marry me, Miss Sarah Maxwell? Will you live with me and be my love?"

A ghost of a smile crossed her lips. "Yes, Andres, of course I —"

He stopped her words with a kiss that warmed and deepened, and when Andres knew it would not be enough he released her. With a slight smile he said, "I can wait now because I know that we have a whole lifetime ahead of us, Sarah." He drew her into his arms and held her in an embrace that spoke not just of passion but of love and of the promises of years to come.

There was a hint of autumn in the air that Sunday afternoon. The patio bloomed with azaleas and chrysanthemums and the sun shone on the sparklets of water from the center fountain.

With the first strummed notes of the two guitars, Doña Teresa turned and smiled at Ellie and Aunt Jo. "It's time," she whispered.

Silvia and Richard came first, smiling self-consciously at each other and the assembled guests as they made their way to a flower bedecked altar where the priest waited. Then, one on either side, they watched as Sarah and Andres came forward.

Her dress was blue, the color that he loved. She carried a cluster of gardenias.

Just for a moment Sarah gazed out beyond the garden and the golden fields to the mountains rising in the distance. Then, as the priest began to speak, she put her hand in Andres's and looking up at him knew that she had come home at last.

Silhouette Special Edition

COMING NEXT MONTH

AN UNEXPECTED PLEASURE—Lucy Hamilton
Cate and Jesse had been childhood friends, but hadn't seen each other for years. Chance brought them together again, seemingly forever. Then betrayal threatened to tear them apart.

HEART OF THE EAGLE—Lindsay McKenna
To ornithologist Dahlia Kincaid, Jim Tremain was like an eagle—dangerous and powerful. But he wasn't the predator he'd first seemed. Could she risk her heart for such a man?

MOMENTS OF GLORY—Jennifer West
Maggie Rand was a proud, wild, mean-tempered woman. Chance Harris knew better than to become involved. But somewhere in those velvet eyes was his future—and he couldn't turn away.

DREAM LOVER—Paula Hamilton
Her script had a message and there was no way Susan McCarthy would let some Hollywood wheeler-dealer twist it into a comedic vehicle for Bruce Powers's massive ego. But Susan had forgotten that Bruce was every woman's fantasy—including hers.

CATCH THE WIND—Caitlin Cross
It was Terminator's last chance—as well as trainer Allegra Brannigan's. Then Scott Charyn returned home to make peace with his father, and Allegra began to feel that she had another chance—this time at love.

TUCKERVILLE REVIVAL—Monique Holden
Tuckerville was a perfect example of a sleepy little town. But the town was fading, and Mayor Rhetta Tucker knew she had to save it. Then Bates McCabe buzzed into town—with a plan that could save them all.

AVAILABLE NOW:

THE ARISTOCRAT
Catherine Coulter

A SLICE OF HEAVEN
Carol McElhaney

LINDSEY'S RAINBOW
Curtiss Ann Matlock

FOREVER AND A DAY
Pamela Wallace

RETURN TO SUMMER
Barbara Faith

YESTERDAY'S TOMORROW
Maggi Charles

Take 4 Silhouette Special Edition novels
FREE

and preview future books in your home for 15 days!

When you take advantage of this offer, you get 4 Silhouette Special Edition® novels FREE and without obligation. Then you'll also have the opportunity to preview 6 brand-new books —delivered right to your door for a FREE 15-day examination period—as soon as they are published.

When you decide to keep them, you pay just $1.95 each ($2.50 each in Canada) *with no shipping, handling, or other charges of any kind!*

Romance *is* alive, well and flourishing in the moving love stories of Silhouette Special Edition novels. They'll awaken your desires, enliven your senses, and leave you tingling all over with excitement...and the first 4 novels are yours to keep. You can cancel at any time.

As an added bonus, you'll also receive a FREE subscription to the Silhouette Books Newsletter as long as you remain a member. Each issue is filled with news on upcoming books, interviews with your favorite authors, even their favorite recipes.

To get your 4 FREE books, fill out and mail the coupon today!

Silhouette Special Edition®

Silhouette Books, 120 Brighton Rd., P.O. Box 5084, Clifton, NJ 07015-5084

**Clip and mail to: Silhouette Books,
120 Brighton Road, P.O. Box 5084, Clifton, NJ 07015-5084** •

YES. Please send me 4 FREE Silhouette Special Edition novels. Unless you hear from me after I receive them, send me 6 new Silhouette Special Edition novels to preview each month. I understand you will bill me just $1.95 each, a total of $11.70 (in Canada, $2.50 each, a total of $15.00), with no shipping, handling, or other charges of any kind. There is no minimum number of books that I must buy, and I can cancel at any time. The first 4 books are mine to keep.

BS18R6

Name _____ (please print)

Address _____ Apt. #

City _____ State/Prov. _____ Zip/Postal Code

• In Canada, mail to: Silhouette Canadian Book Club, 320 Steelcase Rd., E., Markham, Ontario, L3R 2M1, Canada
Terms and prices subject to change.
SILHOUETTE SPECIAL EDITION is a service mark and registered trademark.   SE-SUB-1

**Where passion and destiny meet . . .
there is love**

Jesse's Lady

Veronica Sattler

**Brianna Deveraux had a feisty spirit matched by that
of only one man, Jesse Randall. In North Carolina,
1792, they dared to forge a love as vibrant and alive
as life in their bold new land.**

JES-H-1